a chance at happiness

OTHER INDIAINK TITLES

Anjana Basu	*Black Tongue*
Anjana Basu	*Chinku and the Wolfboy*
Anjum Hasan	*Neti, Neti*
A.N.D. Haksar	*Madhav & Kama: A Love Story from Ancient India*
Boman Desai	*Servant, Master, Mistress*
C.P. Surendran	*An Iron Harvest*
Chitra Banerjee Divakaruni	*The Mirror of Fire and Dreaming*
Chitra Banerjee Divakaruni	*The Conch Bearer*
Haider Warraich	*Auras of the Jinn*
I. Allan Sealy	*The Everest Hotel*
I. Allan Sealy	*Trotternama*
Indrajit Hazra	*The Garden of Earthly Delights*
Jaspreet Singh	*17 Tomatoes: Tales from Kashmir*
Jawahara Saidullah	*The Burden of Foreknowledge*
Kalpana Swaminathan	*The Page 3 Murders*
Kalpana Swaminathan	*The Gardener's Song*
Kamalini Sengupta	*The Top of the Raintree*
Kota Neelima	*Death of a Moneylender*
Madhavan Kutty	*The Village Before Time*
Manohar Malgonkar	*A Bend in the Ganges*
Manohar Malgonkar	*Cactus Country*
Pankaj Mishra	*The Romantics*
Paro Anand	*Weed*
Paro Anand	*No Guns at My Son's Funeral*
Ranjit Lal	*The Life &Times of Altu-Faltu*
Ranjit Lal	*The Small Tigers of Shergarh*
Ranjit Lal	*The Simians of South Block and Yumyum Piglets*
Raza Mir & Ali Husain Mir	*Anthems of Resistance: A Celebration of Progressive Urdu Poetry*
Sanjay Bahadur	*The Sound of Water*
Shandana Minhas	*Tunnel Vision*
Selina Sen	*A Mirror Greens in Spring*
Sharmistha Mohanty	*New Life*
Shree Ghatage	*Brahma's Dream*
Sudhir Thapliyal	*Crossing the Road*
Susan Visvanathan	*Something Barely Remembered*
Susan Visvanathan	*The Visiting Moon*
Susan Visvanathan	*The Seine at Noon*

FORTHCOMING TITLES

Greta Rana	*Hidden Women*
Sanjay Bahadur	*Hul*

a chance at happiness

A book of short stories

Aseem Vadehra

IndiaInk
ROLI BOOKS

IndiaInk
An imprint of
Roli Books Pvt Ltd
M-75, Greater Kailash II Market
New Delhi 110 048
Phone: ++91 (011) 4068 2000
Fax: ++91 (011) 2921 7185
E-mail: info@rolibooks.com; Website: www.rolibooks.com
Also at Bangalore, Chennai, & Mumbai

ISBN: 978-81-86939-65-9
Cover design: Gunjan Ahlawat
Layout design: Sanjeev Mathpal

Typeset in Adobe MrsEaves by Roli Books Pvt Ltd
and printed at Anubha Printers, Noida (UP)

In memory of
Nishit Saran

Mr Alexander

It was a Saturday afternoon. The financial year had just ended and I was more than pleased with the results. We had done well. I had done well. I had attended two meetings in the morning and then taken the day off. I switched off my blackberry and decided to saunter around in Greater Kailash M-block market. Defecting from work was something I had never done, and this felt mutinous and brash. But, I was enjoying spending time in the market where I had hung out as a child with my older sister, intimidated by young men in their open Maruti Gypsy's ogling at her fresh adolescent beauty, oblivious to the shorter, younger me.

Sipping a cappuccino, pondering over the success of my business in the past year and reminiscing about my childhood years in alternate and mixed thoughts, I was lost in contentment.

Everyone around me was at least ten years younger, except for some men in their forties who sat whispering in corners, or straining their eyes at open laptops. The kids – I was pleased with the word – hung around just like I did twenty years ago. The aloofness in their demeanour mirrored the way I had behaved at their age. I marvelled at their flirtatious theatrics, their pearly white smiles as if from toothpaste adverts, tank tops that revealed lace-edged bras and tattooed arms, steps that shuffled with practised abandonment, dangling cigarettes and low-waist jeans that exposed Tommy Hilfiger boxers or brightly coloured panties.

You've come a long way baby, I told myself, repeating the hackneyed phrase in my mind, my foot tapping jovially to Bon Jovi that played in the background.

I sat gleeful, my chest puffed with ego and pride, the smugness apparent in the way I clicked my fingers for another coffee. The waiter looked surprised before his expression turned hurtful, but I continued to look out of the window, basking in my present success and thinking back to a distant past.

Sipping my second cup of coffee, I thought how much I was enjoying the scene around me, the view of the burgeoning chaotic market from the bay window, more intoxicating than the paintings and sculptures I had seen at the Louvre last year.

I remembered the luminosity in Rembrandt's *Bathsheba at her Bath*, and wondered if I was nearly as enraptured by it as the texts and the audio guide insisted I ought to be. I remembered walking around Antonio Canova's *Psyche Revived by Cupid's Kiss*, hypnotized by its beauty, its subtle eroticism, the marble like hardened milk, the movement of the sculpture as fluid as silk in a tempest. I remembered when I walked away from it, I felt like making love. Desperately, urgently. To someone. To anyone. Instead, I relieved myself in the Louvre restroom. But I didn't feel relieved, only temporarily alleviated.

I laughed, thinking about how mixed, muffled and muddled my thoughts were. Drawing from one thought only to teleport to another, the blurred connections, the uninterrupted, though tortuous, flow of my mind. I laughed some more, this time loudly. The teenagers looked at me. I thought I heard one of the prettier girls say, 'Weirdo.'

You've come a long way baby, I repeated to myself again, and then looking towards the girl I said in my mind, *And you don't know the half of it baby*.I felt scornful at my pretentious and banal rebuttal towards her, even if it was only in my mind. I wanted to claw it off. Shuddering at these thoughts, I tried to focus back on Canova's sculpture, but the moment was lost.

At school, my friends were rich. Sons of prosperous businessmen, they went to London and New York for summer vacations and they sported Rolexes and Cartiers in high school. I came from a middle-class family and I would always compare.

I would touch my friend's BMWs like Midas. When shaking hands with them, I would reach a little further and touch the Rolexes and wish they were on my wrist. I never wore a watch in those days, preferring my wrist to be bare rather than wear the Titan my parents had gifted me when I was eighteen.

After I graduated, I began working with a friend who owned a large textile trading business. A-hole-in-the-wall office at the Krishna cloth market in Chandni Chowk gave him two Mercedes and a sparkling gold Rolex. His mother wore the biggest diamonds I had ever seen.

I was burning. I worked with him for two years, learning everything about fabrics, about the trade, about discounts and credits, about yarns, dyes and washes. In two years I was confident to start my own business. When I told him, he shook my hand and wished me well, but I saw betrayal in one eye and his broken heart in the other. I knew we would never be the same again.

I became successful overnight. I knew the business inside out. Customers, suppliers, dealers, bankers – everyone trusted me. I worked hard. I had my targets set on each possession. The watch, the cars, the suits, the shoes, the vacations, the presents, the stationery, the wines, the whiskeys, the apartment.

You don't know the half of it baby, I said in my mind again, and looking at the time on my gold Rolex, I pushed back my chair to leave.

Just as I did, I saw a man enter the glass door, the sweat beads on his bald head immediately evaporating as he entered, the blast of the air conditioner causing the wisps of hair about his ears to vacillate gently. I immediately recognized him, Mr Alexander, my high school teacher. He taught accounts and he was the most loathed teacher in the school. I had never seen him smile, only the slight baring of teeth he gave once during assembly while accepting some bland and eminently forgettable award from the principal.

I debated if I should wish him, but he recognized me with a raise of his brow and slight curve of lips. I was surprised. He shook my hand firmly. It was the first time I shook the hand of any teacher and the warmth and strength of Mr Alexander's hand surprised me further. He smiled and it was far from the snarl I remembered. His cheeks were plump with contentment and his eyes sparkled behind large spectacles.

I didn't know quite what to say, instead bunching together banal questions about school and life.

'Fine,' he said. 'All fine.' He continued smiling, all too aware of my nervousness and childish attempt at conversation. I hemmed and hawed, signalling the end of the conversation, and proceeded to clumsily circumvent his large frame which suddenly seemed to occupy the entire room.

'Join me,' he said. He said it openly without expectation, but it was an invitation nonetheless.

Surprised, slightly annoyed, but wary and reminded of his authority as my former teacher, I sat down resentfully.

'Another coffee?' he said.

'Sure,' I said. Then added, 'Sure, sir. Thank you.'

He smiled again, but this time it seemed as if he was smiling to himself, inwardly happy that the strict life of our all-boys school had me still remember my manners.

He politely signalled a waiter and in an easy, friendly tone asked for two cappuccinos. He said the waiter's name while ordering, reading from the badge that said, 'Hi, I am Pankaj.'

Pankaj, the waiter smiled at him. He was the same waiter I had snapped my finger at earlier.

'So, how is work? I heard you are in garments?' he said.

'Textiles.' I corrected him, but surprised that he was close enough.

As if reading my mind, he said, 'I like to know about my students.' His smile was making me nervous and uncomfortable. I didn't know what to do. The confidence I was bathing in earlier was dissipating, melting like snow under a fierce sun.

'How is it?' he said taking a cookie, munching on it.

'Great, sir. Very good. It's been quite a ride.' I said, trying to be cheery and cool, but finding the words silly and mindless. I felt like kicking myself.

'What about you, sir?' I asked diverting the conversation away from me.

'Retired,' said Mr Alexander. 'Last year,' his tone was jolly and fresh. I continued to be surprised. I thought he would never retire. He had been at our school for forty years and all he did was teach dreaded accounts. And shout and punish. I wondered what he was doing now.

Again, reading my mind he said, 'I am writing a book now. It will be published later this year.' He said happily and contentedly, taking another cookie.

'About what?' I asked curiously. 'About what, sir?' I said again, irritated with myself.

'School, of course. That is the only thing I have known all my life. But not an autobiography. That would be a horror story.' He laughed loudly, crumbs spilling from his thick aubergine lips. His laughter was infectious, so I laughed too, relieved, and the tables near us seemed to smile as well.

The girl who had called me a weirdo earlier turned to give me a flashing, heart-warming smile. She was beautiful.

Mr Alexander saw me stare and the unexpected brightness in my face. He asked, 'Married?'

'No, sir.' It was my turn to laugh loudly, but it was an uneasy laughter, masking the pain of a recent break-up with my girlfriend. 'Who would marry me?' I added ruefully, talking to myself.

'She would,' he said, jerking his head towards the teenage girl.

'Mr Alexander,' I exclaimed. 'She's young enough to be my daughter.' I laughed.

'No,' he corrected me, his tone evocative of our schooling past. 'She's old enough to be my daughter. Never overrate your age, Akshay.'

He remembered my name. I smiled broadly, feeling the wrinkles broaden to my ears. I didn't remember smiling like that in a long time.

'She's quite beautiful,' I said whispering, feeling bold and daring to be telling this to a teacher, especially Mr Alexander.

He nodded and grinned at me.

'Sir,' I said hesitatingly, but gradually settling into the conversation, in this man's cosy and comforting company. 'What do you think of school?'

'You mean to ask me why was I so strict in school?' he said laughingly, his eyes sparkling with gems.

I laughed nervously, fingering the upholstery. 'You were very strict.'

'I loved school,' he said, a little distant, his eyes radiant with memories. 'I think it's important to be strict. It adds the necessary discipline needed later in life.'

'Look at you,' he added. 'A self-made man, aren't you?'

I nodded shyly, pride filling my chest again.

He continued, 'You learnt some of that foundation from your school. Not only from me, but everyone, including Ms Thackeray.'

We both laughed together, my eyebrows rising with shock as well as laughter. Ms Thackeray was the English teacher. She wore low slung saris that exposed her flat, fair midriff, see-through blouses and lacy bras. She was, for every boy in our school the fantasy of many a masturbation, as she was of talk in corridors about her cleavage and red lips.

'So, how are your friends, your famous gang?' he asked.

'Fine, fine,' I said. My mood switched, suddenly dull and defensive.

He didn't say anything, using the pause in the conversation to sip at his coffee and smile at the girl who seemed to be throwing the occasional glance towards us.

'Ashish, Jagat, Gurpreet, Nikhil? There were more...'

'All fine,' I said, this time a little resentfully. But, I was also shocked that he remembered all our names.

I averted my eyes, fixing them deep inside the cappuccino which I slurped noisily.

He changed the subject.

'Any science writing? And drawing?'

I was astonished. How could he know? How could he remember?

'I read your wonderful articles,' he said referring to my work in the school magazine. 'And you drew some lovely illustrations. Very poetic, especially in a subject that isn't considered so, at least at school.' he added.

I smiled weakly. It was a smile that masked thoughts that took me back to what seemed like a million years, a life I had left behind, a life that belonged to someone else. Not Akshay Taneja, Managing Director, Tancja Textiles Private Limited, as my visiting card blared out.

'It's been a very long time, sir. But I did visit the Louvre last year.'

'You're a lucky man to be able to afford such a trip at a young age. And who did you go with?'

I didn't say anything.

'I've begun playing the piano again,' he said breaking the uneasy silence.

'Oh yes,' I said. I had forgotten that he was also the music teacher for the junior school.

'I play in the lobby of Taj Palace every evening from four p.m. to seven p.m.' He said it with pleasure as if stating a fact that gratified him.

'Taj Palace,' I stuttered. That he stated this, without my asking, free of embarrassment and in fact brimming with joy was incredible.

'Yes, isn't it lovely,' he said. 'Such nice people there. I play what I like. It is like meditation.'

I visited Taj Palace innumerable times. It was one of my favourite hotels for leisure and business alike.

Again, uncannily reading my mind he said, 'Yes, I have seen you there many times. You always seem to be lost in many thoughts. You seem to meet people who look very important.'

He continued, 'Then also you look confident, smart, very sure of yourself.'

'Why haven't you come up to me?' I said, in a demanding tone. I lowered my eyes and my voice and said again, 'Why didn't you come up to me, sir?'

He just smiled his contagious smile again, he didn't say anything.

After a pause, I said dejectedly, 'You came to me today.'

'It's not too late, Akshay,' he said. 'Too late for what. Remember that?'

It was one of his favourite quotable quotes amongst many others.

'Pick up your life, son,' he said gently. 'You've got it all, but you need them too.' He pointed at the girl's table where she and her friends were holding their sides, doubling up with gaiety and laughter.

'What was the motto? Our gang, your life?' he said.

'Our gang, my life, my gang, our life,' I said miserably, quoting my gang's motto. I had made that motto.

He reached out and tousled my hair.

'I need to go to my hotel and get into my black tie,' he said with pride and satisfaction. His pride was different from mine. His pride was humble, his pride was a celebration of visited dreams and fulfilled promises.

He paid the bill, insisting that I would get a chance to buy him coffee soon. He hugged me and gave me a kiss on my cheek. I wanted to hold him and cry.

Watching him walk away from the window, I gulped down coffee and torrents of tears as he left me in the market of my childhood, everything racing back to me.

Tara

I loved Tara. I loved the Tabla. And I loved Table Tennis. The weaving dreams of Tara, Tabla and Table Tennis. This was when I was young. Not that I am too old now, but that was a long time ago. Tara ... How did I say her name? Mostly just Tara... But playfully, Stara, Starry, and sometimes Josephine. But only Josephine when I played with her hair, long waves of intertwined wisps of time, silk and dreams that I would carelessly spill all over my face and peak at the golden world that was my life then.

Those days were simple. Briefly simple and I was all too conscious of it. I lived in a four-storey house in Kailash Colony, with its cracked roads and gleaming cars, prosperous fat women haggling with push-cart vendors for vegetables and fruit, businessmen smoking cigarettes and hurrying to their garment factories and real estate businesses.

I would meet Tara after Tabla lessons and before Table Tennis. My hands would be swollen after playing the tabla, the hardened blisters even harder, some peeling to reveal bright young skin, skin that Tara would touch, and I would wince, skin that Tara would kiss, and I would smile. We would gulp badaam milk in Hauz Khaz and I would watch her lips circle the striped straws. Her cheekbones looked even more pronounced then, her eyelashes tickling her eyelids as she looked up at me, her pink mouth biting the striped straw. The bottle would glisten with the emptying milk, and Tara would smile, satisfied, and use her school shirt to wipe the corner of her mouth. Sometimes she would come over, but only thrice a week, time orchestrated to a tune of Tuesdays, Thursdays, and Saturdays. She would come in late afternoon when the house with its four storeys and sixteen members was unusually quiet, the Tabla resting on satin cushions, the Table Tennis racquet lost in the mess of my room, and Tara in my arms. The thin light through green curtains splashed on her young body, casting shadows like a sundial while Tara slept or listened to my stories, or to the Tabla. As I watched her, she would watch me, the colourful print of the sheets seemed to blend into her skin as the hours would bend, curving around time. Sometimes she would hum, and then she was Tara, sometimes she would sing and then she was Josephine. The rhythm of my fingers close to her ears, the movement made the soft young hair around her ears wave and tremble, her eyes watched my concentration, and I would break it with a smile and a kiss on her ear. Her eyelashes were wet in the summer when the air conditioner broke down, delicate beads of sweat framing eyes of kohl and mascara, streaking her cheek, so she looked like a star from an Almodovar movie, and then she became my Stara, but when we made love I only called her Tara. I played and she watched, I spoke and she listened, my arms gesticulating, brushing her lips, her small breasts nestled in my body.

Tara after the Tabla and before Table Tennis.

As the light would fade, and the stirrings of the house began, we would unlock our skin revealing patchy red marks of aroused blood, her undone hair would be quickly made up, my undone jeans changed into grey shorts. We would whizz past my mother and Tara would say a perfunctory hello to my mother's unchanging impassive expression. We would sprint down the steps three at a time. I knew my mother had no particular love for Tara. For her Tara was simply fulfilling her son's teenage appetite.

I didn't think of that much. I had to drop Tara home and avoid the thick rush hour to reach the club to play Table Tennis.

My coach and I would play for as much as three hours and it was seldom ever less than two and a half. I would practice one stroke after another, backhand, forehand, pushing, spins, cuts, chops, smashes, top spins, cross court, down the table, services, one stroke after another, though sometimes it was only one stroke for three hours, and the ball would seem like an object at optical infinity, light streaking from it, like sweat streaking down my shorts, pinching and burning the skin between my thighs, the sharp fragrance of dried semen awakening me to the game, awakening me to Tara.

Taals in the afternoon, one taal after another, the taals of the table and the tabla, the mechanical strokes of repetition, bouncing and striking my fingers, clutching and whipping my wrist, the tabla an extension of my empty hand, the racquet an extension of my Tara-filled hands. In those endless days, it seemed like Tara would be endless. Like we would be endless.

Sometimes I would pick her up from her school; she would be in her white uniform, her skirt box-pleated into long rectangles of starch, the shirt buttoned till her collarbone, the curve of her breast and the beginning of her bra visible when she sat in the car through the split between the buttons. She would lift her hands to tie up her shoulder-length hair, her underarms glistening, a smattering of prickly hair, and I would smile and she would say 'what what,' and I would say 'nothing nothing,' as I placed my hand in her box-pleated lap, the folds swallowing my tired fingers. In the days that I had no Table Tennis or Tabla, the days would be labelled with only Tara, and Tara's wishes. We would watch movies and I would watch her laugh, her lips spreading to make twinkling dimples, the corners of her eyes wreathed in tiny wrinkles, folds of skin that I wanted to get lost in, skin that I delicately kissed.

Sometimes she would watch me play Table Tennis, and my coach with his impressive red turban and greasy beard would belt his trousers tighter so they rose above his ankles and above the faded brown sneakers, and with his knuckles shoved deep in his armpits, and his chest pushed out, he would blink and smile at her.

I would play, cautious not to be impressive, but fierce enough to show my skill. I stood ten inches from the table and moved from one foot to the other, my weight shifting around my hips and the ball made its way tick-tock-thwack across the table, sometimes with soft bounces, sometimes violent, but always with control, and in between shots I wiped my sweating palms against my grey shorts. 'Move, keep moving' ... my coach would say and he would look from me to Tara in quick succession and it seemed like my coach was more distracted by Tara than I was. Tara would never lean against the wall, she stood with her hands by her sides, ready to catch an errant ball, and she would throw me a quick smile as she threw the ball at my coach, never at me, and at the end of the hours her long neck was damp with sweat. I would lean against her when she drove me home when I was especially exhausted, which I almost always was, and I would watch the sweat on her neck cool in the car, the tiny beads of sweat evaporate from the tiny beads of skin that made wonderful patterns against the glittering traffic of evening lights.

When Tara's grandmother, who Tara was especially close to, died later that year, I remembered the glittering lights as I watched the body being cremated, the fire crackling against the wood, the wood cracking against the fire, Tara's face glowing through fiery flames, her face lined with sweat and pouring tears.

A few months later as I finished school and Tara her mourning, I got selected in the Delhi Table Tennis team. She was in the last year of her school, and I was free of school uniforms and books that scared me with their complicated language and menacing numbers. I was free of exams, and I was free to play Tabla and Table Tennis.

Tara always came first in school, she had never come second, and I seldom made it above the bottom five of my class. Although she was a year junior to me, she would try and teach me. She would ask me questions from heavy books and recite mathematical equations like poetry while I played with her hair, making circles on her shoulder, imagining her bra strap as a bridge, tracing its hard satin carving into my Tara's shoulders.

I was ranked only sixteenth in Delhi when I got selected in the team, probably because of the heavy influence of my coach who was in the Association. I didn't care. I knew I was good, and it was worth it to take somebody else's place. That summer Tara got selected as the lead in an inter-city drama competition. She was a born actor, though I thought she was better at debating, and even better, though carelessly so, at running and badminton. She was the lead of an original production called 'Postcards', a play about school life and remembrance. The irony wasn't lost on me. Tara spent hours rehearsing the production, just as I spent hours at Talkatora stadium playing six to eight hours, running up and down concrete stands that ringed the indoor stadium practicing drills and improving my fitness.

That summer, my Tabla faded away after twelve years of riyaz with the same guru. I had seen him lose most of his hair, and whatever left turn into an icy grey, a grey that reminded me of my grey shorts, shorts that I threw away when Tara said I had worn them out. I promised my teacher that it was only temporary and that I would start playing as soon as the Table Tennis season was over. But I could sense betrayal and loss in his shining eyes as he drove away on his scooter that May afternoon. I stood quietly as I watched my tears make small untidy rippled circles on my dusty shoes, and I counted them till the sound of the scooter faded at the turn of the road. That was the last I saw of him, till six years later I saw his smiling face in the obituary section in *The Times of India*, pushed in my face by my mother, who didn't say anything, simply showed it to me. And I stared at his face, angry that he never smiled at me, angry that I never made him smile.

I played Table Tennis with Ishan, who had been in the Delhi team for two years and his sister Pallavi who was her school champion at fifteen and captain of the under-seventeen Delhi team. We trained hard, and there would be seldom any conversation, though between breaks and tired interludes it became obvious to me that Pallavi liked me. She knew I had a girlfriend but it didn't change the way she watched me. It was probably no more than a crush, but at fifteen it could have been deceptively more. I saw Tara less and less. My practice would leave me exhausted and yearning for bed. Even when Tara and

I would find time to be with each other, I would fall asleep, curling away from her, my body aching for her, but more than her, aching for sleep.

Sometimes I saw her at her practice at the hotel which was also the main sponsor of the play and I would get a sense of dread when I approached the banquet hall. Shrieks of laughter and music emanated from the doors, the booming voice of the director ordered stage right! and stage left! and my Tara would be up on the stage, her skilful acting charming everyone, Tara dancing with Shiv, the lead male, dancing to soulful songs of remembrance and love, looking into his deep, sharp eyes, as he twirled her, again and again. Her Starry, Starra, Tara-ness filled the room like springtime, his hips pressed against hers, and could he be erect was all I would wonder as I watched my Tara in a world different from ours, a world different from mine, a world of her own, a world that I was not a part of, a world that I became insanely jealous of. I could only gulp down lumps of unborn tears and I tried to smile watching her dance, again and again.

That summer it seemed like the whole world fell in love with Tara.

I tried to counter by talking of Ishan and Pallavi, but I would be met with sweet nods as her head rubbed against my shoulder, and her eyes only spoke of our love and her trust.

I began to lose my concentration at the table. I would hardly play out five-ten strokes of a practice drill before the ball threw itself in the net, or bounced on the wooden floor. My coach would glare at me, his eyes bulging, the red turban cutting into his skin looking like a peaked mountain as he wiped sweat from his forehead and shouted empty instructions in my burning ears.

One such afternoon, after hopeless play and losing ten games to Ishan and proving yet again to be an inadequate partner, we changed in the locker room. I could sense his anxiety. This wasn't doing anything for his game, this was not why I was chosen to be a training partner. Pallavi suggested a movie to break the tension, and cajoled us into a brighter mood that matched the bright, sunny afternoon outside Talkatora.

I remember her pale pink shirt, slightly see through, and her quick steps dancing on the paved red sandstone in front of the Priya theatre. When Ishan went to get popcorn during intermission, we kissed, quickly, silently, and urgently. And so began steady kisses in empty locker rooms, in the sweating corridors of Talkatora, in the car when I dropped her home. I was sure Ishan knew, but I never thought he would tell Tara.

I continued to meet Tara at her play rehearsals and her hand would be draped about Shiv's shoulder as they lounged with practiced casualness between practices, his confident smile beaming down on her radiating face. My Tara about his arms, my Tara giving him smiles that were only for me, and I could only be glad for Pallavi, even as Tara called out my name and jumped up when she saw me, gaiety and naivety surrounding her, her love unhappily innocent of my pounding jealousy.

When Ishan told Tara three weeks later, he didn't warn me. He didn't tell Pallavi. I had gone to meet Tara after practice and I knew that she knew. She talked to me quietly, Shiv some distance away, a distant but important figure in this melancholy landscape of emotions, and as tears fell from my sorry face, I couldn't say anything. I remember her eyes filled with deep pain, her heartbroken words that sounded like shards of choked phonetics. I fled and found Ishan across the road from the hotel, his arms by his sides, the evening light barely catching his features. I wept on his shoulder, howling Tara's name, pitifully asking for her back. Ishan must have felt disgusted but he didn't betray any emotion even as he held me tight, knowing this was the last time we would embrace.

I never went to practice after that. My coach called me dozens of times and wrote angry letters to me and my parents. He came to my house twice and I feigned inexplicable illnesses. The last I saw him was from my balcony as he slammed the door of his Maruti 800, the red of the car matching the red of his turban and the red of his blazing eyes as he looked up at me with hatred.

My parents weren't concerned. For my father, Table Tennis was a pause of pride before his only son joined the family business. They didn't seem to notice the absence of Tara. I hated them for it. The conversations moved along the comfortable route, of suitable colleges and business growth, punctuated with patronising nods of encouragement.

When I joined the family business four years after studying in the US, my passport and my personality stamped with approving acknowledgement, I heard that Tara was married to Shiv and had two daughters. That first day at work, as my father escorted me to a teak-panelled office I could only blink back memories, staring at my new laptop swirling with proud profits and boastful balance sheets.

A Chance at Happiness

When Amit Gupta discovered that he was not HIV positive, the feeling that rose in his throat and expanded against his ears was of betrayal.

He had spent the last twelve years of his life in doom and terror; his childhood, his adolescence, his teenage years were punctuated and punctured with fear. It seemed like the bravado of the test was in the confirmation of a positive result. A confirmation that the fear he had lived with all these years was worth it. This is what Amit Gupta thought as he stared at the big bold letters: NEGATIVE. He wondered why the alphabet did not start this way. The letters barked at him from the report, insulting the years, violently dismissing them, laughing at his fear, jeering at his cowardice, spitting at his childhood, leering at his fate. The paper was flimsy, serrated at either end with perforated punches on the sides. He stared at the holes, the perforated page, and it reminded him of his anus. Perforated and torn as it had been during those months of abuse. He was not quite sure whether he could really call it abuse without inwardly recoiling that it was as much his doing and sometimes some of it felt so good. But did it? Did it feel good or was this his only way towards acceptance?

Amit was the third child born into an already perfect family of four – his parents and his twin brothers. The twins were six years older than him. He was an accident, as his father liked to joke with friends at the many cocktail parties and dinners they had at their home. Amit remembered his father guffawing gratingly, leaning heavily against the teak-panelled bar which was the centrepiece of the drawing room, so that when he stood behind it, he looked to Amit Gupta like the tallest man in the world.

He could picture those cocktails now, as he stood outside the pathology clinic, a blazing, unkind sun scorching down on him and on an already blackened Delhi. His father's white hair slicked back, the silk pocket square bloomed with practiced casualness from the dinner jacket, his ivory hands delicately swirled the crystal stirrer in the golden whiskey, a glowing cigarette, his voice authoritative and patronizing, his lush moustache turned at the edges, the sparkling diamond on his right ring finger bounced shards of light from the Murano chandelier. His mother with her coy expression, her silk saree embracing her delicate frame, standing an arm's length from her husband at the corner of the bar, her upturned face and three quarter look of adoration towards her husband, her hip angled away, so she looked like a dancing odalisque striking a pose for her king. His brothers, on the other side of the bar, confident and self assured in tailor-made khakis, neat powder-blue shirts, and delicately combed hair. His father would hold the twins' heads in his hands and ruffle their silken hair as if stroking lions on a throne. In this perfect family portrait, Amit wouldn't know where to stand and he would lose his way through the many guests, the forest of legs, pleated trousers, and draped silks.

The enormous drawing room was a playground for Amit. He hid behind tusser silk drapes and bright tafetta sofas, driving model cars up and down imitation Chippendales, constructing Lego on intricate Kashmiri carpets while the goddess Lakshmi glowered at him from a corner, standing on a lotus, her four arms splayed, her majestic crown pressed with gold leaf and precious stones, her breasts bronze and hard, her erect nipples with concentric circles, nipples he wonderingly stared at, nipples which he sacrilegiously touched.

It started when Amit was twelve.

One sweltering afternoon after school, when the table was cleared of the Wedgewood plates, the mahogany wiped clean of dahi and daal, his mother retired to her room for the customary nap, and the twins out to Khan Market as they were every day, gelling their hair and sporting oversized Polo T-shirts; the house was quiet, and the dog was asleep, his tongue taking in the coolness of the white Macarana marble, as Amit continued to sit at the table doing his homework.

The cook, who was clearing the table, made clowning faces and Amit laughed. They got along. Amit was friendly with all the servants of the house. Staff, he liked to call them, quite proud of his political correctedness at such a young age. Servants, his parents insisted. He often played cricket or football with them in the long driveway. It was awkward to treat them like mere servants.

He felt embarrassed when the twins clapped for their attention, and deeply ashamed when he saw his father slap them for adding too much salt in his food or forgetting to clean the blue Mercedes. Once, at dinner when the cook was serving rice, he had dared to ask why the servants ate a different kind of rice. 'It looks dirty,' he said. The twins hollered in laughter, his mother looked embarrassed and his father frowned dangerously. The cook must have understood the English, because he receded hastily, bowing and ashamed. Years on, Amit Gupta could never eat rice without thinking of that dinner.

That sweltering afternoon the cook lingered, continuing his pantomime. He asked what Amit was studying, he asked casual questions, and through jokes and encouraging expressions he asked if Amit knew what an erection was.

'Of course I know,' Amit said, almost scoffing, but was instantly curious at the brazen nature of this question, a question from a servant. A question that seemed even more vulgar and erotic in Hindi.

The cook slid his coarse hands through Amit's hair and the back of his neck and asked if he could see it. Mumbling, unsure, aroused and afraid, Amit said yes, and the cook, without wasting time or precious opportunity, quickly unzipped Amit's shorts and rubbed at his erection, pulling at the penis, the spidery, bristly beginnings of pubic hair glistening from the bus ride home. He tugged and pulled, all the while making clowning faces at Amit, who twirled the pencil in hand, almost acting as if nothing was happening – surprised, aroused and curious. The cook pulled out his own penis – an adult penis, the first sexual organ Amit had ever seen – and shock, disgust and fear swirled in his young brain The cook pushed back the foreskin, a bead of semen formed at the tip as the penis was forced upon Amit's face with a guttural instruction to kiss it. He did. Again, said the cook. He did. Again and again. He stood Amit up and pulled the white shorts down and pushed against him, not quite penetrating him, but pushing repeatedly, mimicking, perhaps afraid to fully insert himself, perhaps because withdrawal takes time, perhaps because he could walk away quickly if he heard the creak of the front door, perhaps afraid that a child's scream would echo through the house. Drops of blood streaked down from Amit's anus, staining his thighs, falling on the Kashmiri carpet where the patterned hungry tufts of wool and silk swallowed them whole.

Later that day at dinner, Amit found it difficult to sit and his hands trembled on the folded napkin on his lap. The aroma of saffron and spices from the kitchen sickened him, the hum of the pressure cooker pressed against his temples, the footsteps of the cook, and the secret clowning faces he continued to make as he dropped hot chapattis into a basket of weaved gold set the clock of fear in him.

In the bathroom mirror he bent down and saw his anus clearly for the first time. An asterisk, he thought. And then quietly, a small drop of blood appeared, becoming larger and larger till it dropped into the canvas belt of the shorts around his ankle.

For months that seemed like epic journeys, this continued: the mimicry of sex in different positions, the big body above him, the blackened lips that tasted of morning cooking and beedis, the hissing breath of arousal that came through hairy nostrils, the hard hands that left marks of trapped blood all over his young skin. Amit Gupta would see the Goddess Lakshmi angry in her corner, and he was deeply ashamed for enjoying being rubbed, averting his eyes and praying for forgiveness.

Sometimes the cook would take Amit down to the garage – a makeshift servant's room, which was always empty in the afternoon – and he would masturbate urgently, showering the tiled walls of the stinking bathroom with semen, all the while pushing and pulling at Amit's penis violently, urging him, violating him.

What should I know? Where will I stop, he thought. He contemplated telling his mother, but he could already hear her wails and shrieks in his mind. He shuddered at the thought. Telling the twins or his father was impossible. He tried timidly to avoid the cook. A week or so of success would be met later with erotic forcefulness that left him raw and nearly torn.

Then one day, close to the Diwali break, Amit came back home to find his mother in the kitchen, cooking calmly, with a certain air of irritation about her. Amit was terrified, and trying to keep his voice neutral, he enquired about the cook. His mother told him that he had been thrown out. He had seemed unwell these past few weeks, and they had sent him to the family doctor a week ago, who, upon conducting tests, had diagnosed him as HIV positive.

She added menacingly that frustrated servants in the city with wives in villages had nothing better to do at night but visit red light areas. Red-light areas. I am a red light area, he thought.

There was no penetration. Not full penetration anyway. He tried to reason with himself. That day, and then every day for twelve years.

Every day became a day of survival. In the mornings as he readied for school, the reflection in the mirror stared mockingly at him. Time became hollow. Every bout of flu, fever, diarrhoea, and common ailments became the well of death. Routine blood tests became nightmares of reality. At night he would twist and turn, sweating in his white kurta pyjama, bitterly awake, only to see a hopeless dawn seep in through faded jacquard curtains. He had read that HIV could take ten years, sometimes more, to awaken, to spread, to ravage the body slowly. Time became a series of punctuation marks. And that is how he viewed it. School exams would be considered semi colons, when his mind was more occupied to clear his grade. Table tennis was dot dot dots, as the ball bounced from one side of the table to the other, his furious playing allowing him to become captain of the school team and to forget temporarily about disease and death. These were brief interludes, gasps of normal life, parenthesis of teenage angst that he coveted hungrily, lapping up every small experience, recording his life in piles of diaries. Sorrows, joys, happiness, sadness existed in a space of magnetic repulsion, a space below horror and fear, which simmered constantly like burning oil in the young folds of his brain.

He refused to make love to his first girlfriend at sixteen. She was the prettiest girl in school, and even as she begged him naked, her young breasts caressing his stomach, her tears of rejection filling his navel, he laughed, nervous and neurotic, and begged her for patience. He promised her that time would bring them to it. But promises clanged like empty vessels and a year later when she cheated on him, he wasn't surprised or angry. He was relieved and heartbroken, his heart cleaving cleanly down the middle, a heart that would never be whole again.

Time was winking at him, his birthdays winked at him, sneaking up from behind, each cake baked by his mother with the flames of years to be blown away, a step closer to death. Six months before he turned nineteen, as soldiers died valiantly in the Kargil war, the newspapers hollering obsessive patriotism, the family moved to a new house, a larger house; more space was needed, his mother informed him. They were eagerly seeking brides for the twins. Boastfully she proclaimed that offers from families were pouring in from all over the world – Australia to America, Punjab to Mumbai.

On his nineteenth birthday, at the new house, he thought menacingly, bitterly, that he was only seven. Seven years since he had enjoyed his servant. Yes, I enjoyed it, his voice screamed inside him, racing, zig-zagging, cutting through all other reality, as he blew the candles, the swirling smoke blurring the faces of cheering friends and family, turning away to their cocktails and conversations.

Amit wished he could join the army. If he died in war, it would be noble, far and opposite from the ignobility of dying of AIDS. But he didn't go to war, and it was just a joke around the table when he announced his decision to join the army in an uncertain, pleading manner. The twins as usual roared with laughter-an expression he wrote on his bedroom wall-an expression that reminded him of Enid Blyton books. The discussion moved to suitable brides.

A joke, just like the title of Assistant Vice President that his father and brothers chose for him at their automotive parts company. A suitable title for the owner's youngest son, a suitable title for the hypocrisy of family businesses that pretended to be professional to please their Japanese counterparts.

A few years later, now, as he looked at his test results, Amit Gupta, assistant vice president and HIV negative, chose to drive to his old home. He rolled down the window of his Land Cruiser and peered through the wrought-iron gates adorned with brass filigree, and he saw three children, seven or eight years old: two girls and a boy playing cricket with the servants of the house. The mother was surely asleep and their father flying in starched skies above. He prayed for a chance at happiness to the empty bronze gods and drove on.

A Date in Paharganj

'Only SpiceJet available at 6.50, sir. Everything is sold out,' said Rita in her sweet trembling voice. She knew her boss would not be happy travelling a budget airline.

'Are you sure?' asked Ankit Kejriwal irritably. 'Have you checked with all our agents?'

'Yes sir. Sorry sir. You are booked for tomorrow...'

'I know. I know. But the meeting is over. What do I do? Stay here another day?'

'Sorry sir,' said Rita, longing, trying to please the boss she never could please.

This was the exchange between secretary and boss on a Saturday evening when it was the end of winter in Delhi, the warmth of March enveloping into a deficient February. But Ankit Kejriwal was in Chennai, where it was already much too hot for his liking. Such weather only suits the south of France or the Bahamas, he thought, not this city, this city of sweat, jarring accent and leather sandals. He smirked, smoking a cigarette in the lobby of the Taj Coromandel.

He had lied to Rita. The meeting was not over as he had told her, it had been altogether cancelled. It was a fact he didn't want to reveal to Rita. She would tell everyone at office. Dad would come to know as well and then there would be hell at home, he thought.

Ankit Kejriwal's business was in home furnishings, one of the many medium-sized businesses that crowded a market already competing desperately with each other. They were no match against Vietnam and China that had diminished their business to a third of what it was just ten years back. Ankit had joined his father four years ago, but he had failed to bring in any new business, a fact that was noticed by all his employees and pointed out directly by his father.

'You wine and dine at every opportunity. But business is the bottom line,' said his father, twirling a moustache more suited for the position of a Colonel than a businessman. It was true that Ankit loved entertaining agents and their foreign buyers. He was especially proud to walk in with them at Oberoi or Taj, letting their white skin and freckled bodies walk respectfully ahead, their oversized sunglasses pushed back on blonde heads. He would order twenty thousand rupee wines, always pointing at the tilted menu so the buyer would get a glimpse of the price of the bottle. But scarcely did the buyers provide more business, instead often insisting on further discounts on already established prices.

In Chennai, Ankit was to meet a buyer from China, who wanted to do collaborative business. Ankit was excited at the proposition. At his arrival in Chennai, much to his dismay he discovered – by way of a message waiting at his hotel – that the buyer had already departed from Chennai early morning. It didn't give any explanation.

And now I am stuck in this shithole, he thought.

He had called Rita two hours later, careful to measure time while sipping tea, eating muffins and smoking cigarettes. Ankit didn't like to travel for business, and the dislike was only alleviated for a few hours spent in the pampering care of a familiar business-class cabin.

Two and half hours in that tube, he thought. Worse, only a middle seat was available.

When he entered the airline purposefully from the front even though the ground staff had advised him that his was one of the last seats, he arrogantly told a cabin crew member that he wanted to sit on an aisle as upfront as possible.

'Sir, I am so sorry. The flight is completely sold out,' she said flashing her best professional smile.

'That is why I don't travel your airline. Terrible service.' He huffed as he walked on, his Louis Vuitton duffel bag grazing and bumping the elbows of seated passengers without care.

When he reached his row, twenty-one, he found the other seats already occupied. The middle seat looked pitifully small for his podgy frame. The man on the window seat was undoubtedly a Chennai native, thought Ankit, his ebony skin gleaming against the rusty glow of the setting sun. He was dressed shabbily in worn-out jeans and a faded shirt. His feet were in the characteristic black leather sandals. The man at the aisle was fairer, dressed in a checked blue shirt and khakis. He was turning the newspaper through rimless reading glasses. Probably a software engineer from Delhi, thought Ankit. It didn't take him long to weigh his options.

'Excuse me,' he said to the Chennai native, putting on an American accent that he spoke in when he was with his foreign buyers, 'I would like to sit at the window please.'

'If you don't mind,' he added, expecting appreciation at condescension.

'Sir,' said the thin man in a strong Tamil accent, looking at him with sharp, beady eyes, 'This is my seat. I would like to sit here.' And he held his boarding pass up for inspection.

Ankit looked at the man on the aisle seat, the obvious north Indian sheathed in his cream skin. He peered interestedly back at him. There was already a small queue beginning to form behind and in front of Ankit. Upon realizing with disdainful reluctance that he was not receiving any support, he took the middle seat with much demonstration of heavy breathing and tongue clicking.

I must tell Swati about this experience, he thought, settling into his seat, deliberately letting the flap of the seat belt cross into the lap of the man from Chennai.

Swati was Ankit's fiancée. They were to get married in two weeks. He had met her exactly four times prior, and only twice alone. Their parents had matched them three months earlier through a wedding broker who took a sum of two lakh from Ankit's father to make the match certain.

Ankit saw her for the first time when his family was invited for tea. In the ceremonial gaiety that surrounded them Swati and Ankit had hardly spoken a word to each other. The lavish room of dancing marble Krishnas adorned in gold and silk cocooned them on this evening of indenture, a deal for life, a match made under the auspices of brokers, net worth, community, and a blue Casanova god.

Ankit was disappointed that she was not as fair as he had imagined, or as her resume had proclaimed. No doubt, he thought, the portfolio shots in the impressive silk folder that he had flipped through had been photoshopped. But her face was oval and her features certainly not bland. Her long eyelashes framed eyes of virtuousness. Her silky straight hair whisked above liberal breasts.

She's pretty, yes she is pretty, he thought as the plane pushed back gently. His thoughts leered to the erotic as he remembered the last time they had met, only two days ago, when he had kissed her hungrily for the first time, his hand probing her crotch, his mouth wide open as he swallowed her lips. Her tongue was certainly enthusiastic, he thought.

These thoughts brought a small bump in his trousers of fine wool and he pushed his hands between his legs and fell asleep before take-off.

As the aircraft took wings, his head rested peacefully on the gaunt shoulder of his Chennai compatriot and the two men at either side of a snoring Ankit smiled at each other. He woke at the very end of the journey, and wiped the drool on his lips and chin with the back of his hand. He looked at his watch, a gigantic gold Audemars Piguet – a present from his to be in-laws – and was pleased to see the flurry of runway lights racing to meet the quickly descending aircraft.

Everyone got up as soon as the plane came to a gentle halt. Bending his neck to avoid knocking his head on the overhead storage, he waited impatiently as the flight slowly cleared out. Just as he was walking to the rear which had emptied out faster than the front, he saw a foreigner – a white woman – struggling to lift her bag from the storage. The prickly hair on her underarm stirred in him a familiar sensation. Always ready to accommodate a foreigner, especially a woman, he lifted her bag easily.

'Thank you,' said the woman gratefully, in a European accent. She was probably in her late thirties, her skin was lightly speckled, her eyes large and emerald green.

'You are welcome,' said Ankit in his American accent. They nodded smiles at each other and exited the plane.

At the baggage carousel, he intentionally took his place next to her.

'So, where are you from?' he said, his accent varying from Indian to American.

'Italy,' she said in a charming accent. 'And you, are you from America?'

'No, no,' he laughed embarrassed. 'I am from here, New Delhi. I go to America for work.'

'I studied in college in the US,' he added.

'I thought you were American,' she laughed pleasingly. 'Sorry.'

'That is okay. Many people in Delhi have an international accent,' he flaunted, satisfied with the choice of his words. She nodded and the short straw-coloured hair that had bleached in the Indian sun bobbed gently.

She was of slight built, petite for a European, he thought. Her T-shirt skimmed above the waist of her cargo pants, her stomach visible as she knotted her hair in a small pony. Her nipples were visibly erect in the cool temperature of the Delhi airport. When her backpack arrived, he chivalrously lifted it for her.

'Thank you,' she said smiling at him. 'Your bag?' she enquired.

'Should be here any moment. I made them put a priority tag on it,' he lied.

'Oh, that is nice. I didn't know budget airlines in India offered such services.'

'Everything at a price in India, you know,' he laughed. 'Here it is,' he said picking up a Louis Vuitton bag matching his duffel.

'Louis Vuitton!' she exclaimed. 'Original?'

'Of course,' he said unabashed. 'Of course.' He repeated.

'Beautiful,' she said. 'Beautiful.' She repeated.

As they walked together towards the exit, he asked, 'Are you in Delhi for long?'

'A few days. And then back to Italy.'

'My name is Ankit,' he said. 'Ankit Kejriwal.'

'Annalisa,' she said warmly, shaking his hand. What an exotic name, he thought. Like a stripper.

'So where are you staying, may I ask?'

'At Hotel Rak International.'

He hadn't heard of it. 'Where is that?' he asked curiously.

'Paharganj,' she said taking her time to pronounce the word.

'Oh! Must be adventurous!' he said. She looked at him quizzically.

Overlooking her expression he said, 'Are you taking a taxi?'

'No, much too expensive. I will find out about buses.'

They had nearly reached the exit. He had little time to make a decision that had already been brewing in his mind since they had been waiting at the carousel. 'I'll drop you,'he said.

She laughed, a pretty sound. 'No thank you. That is too much.'

'No, it is nothing. And Delhi is not like Chennai. It is very cold here.' His hands unconsciously gestured towards her breasts, 'The bus will be very cold.'

'Really? Are you sure? Are you sure it is not out of the way for you?'

Ankit couldn't believe his luck. He had expected her to say no. Not to trust strangers in a foreign land. But, I suppose I look well-meaning and, well, rich. He straightened his shoulders.

'No, no,' he said. 'Not at all out of the way.'

'Thank you so much. Thank you.' She smiled at him gratefully with tired eyes.

Ankit's driver, a tall man with a moustache that mimicked Ankit's father's moustache, stood waiting in a spotless white uniform punctuated with thick brass buttons. He had worked for the Kejriwal family for the past twenty-three years. When he was employed, Ankit was two years old, and over the years, the child who ran into his arms after school had turned into a man that barely acknowledged his handsome salute and folded hands of greeting.

Ankit passed his bags to the driver with insensible ease.

Ankit spoke to him in rapid Hindi, 'Mishra, drop me first. Then this woman to her hotel. Paharganj she says.'

She looked at them with interest as Ankit opened the door of the Honda Accord for her. 'Thank you,' she said.

'I have just received a message,' he lied, looking at his phone, 'that I must go home for a meeting. My father is waiting.'

'Oh!' said the woman, motioning to leave the car.

'No, no,' he said, 'that is not what I meant. I will get off first and then he,' pointing at Mishra, 'will drop you to your hotel.'

'Are you sure?'

'Yes, yes,' his voice was evidently impatient.

Thankful for the ride, she chose to nod and smile, adjusting her shoulders in the comfort of the leather, unused to such comforts in her travels.

The car weaved through the evening traffic with expertise and they sat in momentary silence.

'How come you visited Chennai?' he asked.

'To visit Tirupathi,' she replied. 'It was very beautiful,' she said her voice genuinely excited.

'Have you been there?' she asked.

'We go to Salasirji,' he said. 'Have you heard of that?'

She shook her head.

He nodded. 'My father is a patron. He donates a lot of money to their trust.' He said it indifferently, with a hint of revulsion.

'You must be very rich,' she said admiringly. The streetlights of Delhi made flashing patterns on their faces.

He laughed.

'What are you planning to see in Delhi?'

'Tomorrow, I will see Jama Masjid,' she said. 'And Chandni Chowk,' she said, pronouncing the names hesitatingly and carefully.

'Yes, Chandni Chowk.'

He continued. 'Your knowledge of India is very good.'

'Thank you. Lonely Planet,' she said laughing. Her laughter tingled pleasantly against the back of his ears.

'We buy fabric from there. You know, for my business.'

'Why don't you come?' she said. 'I would like to treat you to lunch for all this help,' her voice was sincere.

He looked at her in surprise; surprise at what he thought was a bold offer, but astonished because this was the first time a girl had asked him out for lunch. Indeed, he himself never had never asked a girl out. A date, he thought breathlessly.

'Oh, I am sorry. Perhaps you are already quite busy.'

'Yes,' he said automatically. 'No,' he said contradicting himself immediately. 'That would be nice. Yes, I will come.' He added animatedly. 'I have not been there in many years.'

'Wonderful. Why don't you come to the hotel at eleven? It is very close from there I hear.'

He was uncertain of that but she seemed to know what she was talking about. He nodded.

When they turned towards his farmhouse, a sprawling estate at the edge of South Delhi, he instructed Mishra to stop at the house gate and not drive in. He didn't want anyone to see the woman. Mishra raised his eyebrows but kept silent. The car stopped outside the gates of broad Burma teak planks.

'See you Annalisa,' he said hurriedly, wanting the car to depart quickly.

'Thank you, thank you so very much. See you tomorrow morning.'

'Yes, yes,' he said as he stepped out of the car. He quickly went across to the driver's side, and said to Mishra in a low voice, 'I want you to come tomorrow morning at ten. But don't mention her, you understand.' And with that he slipped him thousand rupees. The next day was Sunday, Mishra's weekly day off, but a thousand rupee would buy his Sunday as also his silence.

The next morning at the table his parents were having breakfast, both dressed in robes of quilted silk.

'I am going to the gym,' Ankit announced.

His parents looked at him with equal surprise. His mother laughed adoringly, 'You hardly manage to go in the week. You have just come from a hectic trip. It is Sunday. Have a rest.'

'You are getting married in two weeks,' she added triumphantly. 'Why don't you rest,' she repeated.

Which means, he thought gleefully, that he didn't have to spend much time at work. There would be preparations to be made, last minute clothes alterations, presents to be professionally packed, and decorations to be carried out to perfection. The wedding had to be talked about. He had better check on the reporters, he thought.

'Yes Mom, that is true,' he said looking at his father who had returned to the morning paper. 'But that is why I want to go to the gym.'

'To look fit for the wedding,' he added.

'Rome wasn't built in a day,' his father said dryly. It was his favourite proverb and scarcely a week went by when Ankit didn't hear his father say it in exactly the same tone.

'Let him be,' his mother said looking lovingly from husband to son.

'See you soon,' he said touching his parents' feet as his mother passed an affectionate hand over his head and his father patted him about his cheek. 'Your mother is right. You must rest. Well, go on.' Ankit accepted his words gratefully.

He touched the pink Macarana feet of the laughing baby Krishna in his silver swing. The puja room was embellished with silks and precious stones and Ankit muttered a quick word of prayer and a plea for forgiveness before piously touching a dot of saffron paste on his forhead.

In the car, he sat in the front seat, and before a word of greeting to Mishra, he gave him another thousand rupees. He protested silently, but Ankit was already fidgeting with the CD changer.

'To her hotel,' he said nonchalantly. 'How is it?'

'Not exactly your kind of place I should say,' Mishra replied haltingly.

'Tell me Mishra,' he said, 'this Jama Masjid, can I go there?' He continued, 'You know...' he stopped.

'Sir, your parents would not appreciate this at all. I don't think...'

Ankit interrupted impatiently, but his voice trembled, 'Just tell me Mishra, can we as Hindus go?'

'I believe we can, sir,' the driver swallowed. 'I don't think we should. It is not right for us. For you. For you from this family. Your parents...'

'Yes, sure,' said Ankit dismissively, 'just don't tell them anything, okay?' he said waving his arm back towards the house.

Mishra nodded silently, his face knotted with distress.

Even on a Sunday morning, it was a forty-minute drive and when Ankit reached, he thought he was in a new city.

The main bazaar of Paharganj was opposite the New Delhi railway station and it was an untidy picture of rickshaws, peddlers, beggars, travel agencies, car rentals, budget hotels, and shops which sold everything from fedoras to foreign exchange. The road was blocked to cars.

'How do I go?' he demanded.

'By rickshaw, sir. Last night, I...'

But Ankit was already slamming the door shut. He asked a rickshaw puller if he knew the hotel.

The rickshaw puller looked at him through his beedi smoke and in that look Ankit knew that he was the foreigner here, not Annalisa.

Hotel Rak International was in 6-Tooti, a cul-de-sac just off the main bazaar road. It was surprisingly quiet.

Annalisa was already waiting at the reception. He could see her through the spangled geometry of coloured glass on the entrance door of the hotel. Her straw coloured hair was hidden under a broad hat, undoubtedly bought from one of these shops, he thought. She was dressed modestly for Jama Masjid, as advised by the Lonely Planet. Her green top was full sleeved and a woollen sweater was tied about her waist. Her jeans were faded but did not have any holes or tears.

'Hello! Good morning,' she said cheerfully.

'Hi,' Ankit replied, wondering what he was doing here. He looked around the tiny reception area. He thought it would be seedy, that is what he had expected it to be, but it wasn't. It was more or less clean, though he noticed with almost perverse satisfaction that the upholstery of the lone waiting sofa was worn out and dark with grime.

'You are much too kind,' she said, not noticing his inquisitive expression. 'Your house was so close to the airport and you made Mr Mishra drop me all the way here. That was too much. For this, I will treat you both to lunch.'

Alarmed by her alacrity to treat not only him, but the driver as well, Ankit quickly said, 'Don't worry about that.'

The drive to Jama Masjid was short and they were soon surrounded by the systematic chaos of old Delhi. Ankit insisted that Mishra accompany them. Annalisa thought this was a perfectly normal and obvious gesture, but it stemmed from Ankit's fear and revulsion.

The three of them crammed together in a rickshaw and in the bumpy ride, Ankit's elbow kept nudging against the softness of Annalisa's breast. He was slightly disappointed when they finally stopped at the busy Sunday market in front of Gate 2, Jama Masjid.

They made their way between rows of shanty makeshift shops selling shoes, belts, underwear, bras, perfumes, carpets, sunglasses, toys, utensils, and numerous other products.

Ankit looked around in disbelief and astonishment at the plethora of activity. He walked as if in slow motion and was elbowed this way and that by the hurrying crowds, crowds that were enjoying their Sunday, but crowds for whom the Jama Masjid bazaar was a place for bargain and trade.

Ankit saw Hindu women easily distinguishable with the red sindoor in their hair, the Muslims men in the skull caps, and the women in the burkhas, but in the thousands around him with no apparent display of religious affiliation, he found himself, as possibly Muslim as he was Hindu.

On that day the sun was strong, and Ankit looking around at all that was new to him fingered the gold Krishna pendant against his chest not with nervousness but with sublime joy. Years later, he would remember that moment as his one moment of deliverance, of freedom.

He smiled at Annalisa and at Mishra with a newfound, if temporary, benevolent confidence and said, 'Let's go inside,' pointing towards the rows of stairs that led to Gate 2, Jama Masjid.

He hired a guide at the entrance who in impeccable Urdu asked them to remove shoes at the entrance. He translated to Annalisa, whispering, 'They speak poetry. We speak Hindi.' He noticed that he had said it with pride, and he was pleased with his vague compliment, his uneasy secularism.

They learnt that Gate 2 was the east gate, which was the royal entrance, where the kings entered from. The guide pointed to the Red Fort that spread expansively behind them and spoke in a English that mixed all the accents he had heard from tourists visiting from around the world. He told them that Jama Masjid was the largest mosque in India, built by the great Mughal emperor Shah Jahan. It was completed in 1656 and that it took six thousand workers six years to make. It cost a sum of fifteen lakh at that time, and this did not include the cost of the stone which was provided free by various kings in Rajasthan. That is where I am from, Ankit thought.

The low, respectful voice of the guide trailed distantly as Ankit looked around him in wonder, as if entering Disneyland. He looked at the tall minarets meant for the call of the muezzin for *azaan* and the inlay work in the ornamented marble slabs under his feet, each perfectly rectangular like a prayer carpet. Even barefoot there was something sacrilegious about feet in this place, he thought. Twenty-five thousand people gather here on Eid, Ankit heard the guide say, this time a touch of snobbery and reverence mingling with his soft blend of accents.

Ankit looked at the praying men, the way they touched their ears, bowed and kneeled repeatedly. He saw the women who stood outside the main area, their heads bowed deep, their lips moving in prayer. Children ran playfully across the scorching courtyard. Homeless men slept in foetal position in cool corners, yet their position was reverent, as if even in sleep they were grateful for the cool shelter of a merciful God.

The signages were in English, German, French, Spanish and Italian, and Annalisa exclaimed prettily as she read her native language. They climbed the south tower, all one-hundred-and-thirty steps of it, laughing as they chased each other in the spiral of steps, brushing past other tourists and locals in the two-foot wide staircase. When they reached the top, laughter gave way to gasps of wonder as they marvelled at the wide expanse around them.

They were alone. They stood close, their hips touching, his shoulder grazing hers as he pointed out the familiar sights around him. 'Connaught Place,' he exclaimed. He made up names of buildings so she wouldn't move away.

In the coolness of the stone-ensconced tower that protected them from the fiery irreverent sun, Ankit mustered all his courage and reached to kiss Annalisa. They kissed, their lips fused like Old and New Delhi, as indistinct and indistinguishable in the far reaches of the sun-splashed horizon.

Mishra was squatting, warily keeping an eye about him when Ankit and Annalisa came through the entrance and he noticed the spring in his boss's step and the flushed cheeks of Annalisa. He knew this was the beginning of trouble.

'I have to take you home,' said Ankit.

'What about my promise for lunch?' said Annalisa.

He shook his head. Swati had already called him twice, and soon his parents would wonder where he was.

'I have to go Annalisa,' he said apologising.

'It is quite all right. Thank you so much.'

He offered to drop her to the hotel but she shook her head almost sadly, as if all too aware of the impermanence of the sudden romance.

'Goodbye Ankit,' she said and before he could say something she leaned and kissed him on both cheeks. Ankit felt the wetness of her lips and the mixed glares of those who noticed. Mishra let out an audible click in his cheek. 'Goodbye Mr Mishra,' she added brightly.

'Goodbye,' said Ankit.

'Bye,' said Mishra clearing his throat.

At work the next day, Ankit could think of nothing but Annalisa, the way her breast had pressed against his elbow in the rickshaw, the way her lips had felt on his mouth. He thought about her free gaiety, her knowledge about his country, the way she called his driver Mr Mishra.

So different from Swati, he thought. So much more interesting. He could barely spell his thoughts.

She makes me feel alive, yes, she makes me feel alive, he thought, happy with the choice of his words, even though the thought disturbed him.

When he could bear it no longer, he searched the internet, without hope, for the hotel's website or phone number.

There is no way a Paharganj hotel would be listed, he thought.

To his surprise he found the official website instantly. He called the hotel, but she was out. He left his phone number and a simple message, 'Call when you can.' Restless, he waited all day for the phone to ring but it did not. He wondered whether she did not want to call him or if she was out sightseeing in some stupid monument.

At night, after dinner, he was smoking in his bathroom when he heard the trucks from the wedding planners. He could hear the laughter of the workers who were unloading the various paraphernalia for the cocktail party. A cocktail party without cocktails, he thought spitefully.

'In our community, we cannot serve alcohol in public. It is against our tradition and an insult to our elders,' his father had replied when Ankit had argued feebly.

His mother had nodded sagely, her pink lips pursed in a thin line of pious seriousness.

His father continued, contradicting himself, 'But I am modern. We will have a bar in one of the rooms inside the house. For our VIP guests and foreign buyers. It is important Ankit, that you do not tell anyone about it without asking me.' And that was his father's conclusion.

Lost in these thoughts, he jumped when the phone rang.

'Hello,' he said, trying to keep his voice casual.

'Hello Ankit!' Annalisa said in her excited and happy voice.

He didn't know what to say but she steered the conversation easily, telling him about Red Fort, Old Fort and Janpath. He only half listened to what she was saying, lost in her delicious accent, the animated phonetics, the soft sound of her breath when she paused between sentences.

Suddenly he said, as if he could bear it no longer, 'Shall we meet tomorrow?'

'I am eager to meet,' she said. Eager. That sounded like the perfect word to Ankit. A word he would always remember her by whenever he heard it. They agreed to meet at noon at her hotel.

The next morning Mishra tried to reason with Ankit as they drove out. Ankit was distractedly looking at the workers setting up the tents. The workers were perched dangerously, but confidently, like monkeys on high poles, shouting for rope and fabrics, as they strung one bamboo to the next, making a dome like structure.

'Look at all this,' he said, 'you are getting married next week, sir.' He said 'sir' pointedly.

'She's just a friend, Mishra. You relax,' he muttered. 'And if anyone calls your phone, say I am in a meeting with the fabric supplier in Okhla.'

He reached Paharganj early and rang her from the reception.

'Oh, you are here. I will take ten minutes. Come on up to Room 307.'

The receptionist was a bored, unfriendly man. Indifferently, he pointed at the steps. He ran up the three flights of staircase.

He was breathless and nervous when he knocked. The corridor was narrow. She opened the door. She was perfectly ready, he noted almost disappointed, expecting her to be in a bathrobe with wet hair.

He looked inside curiously. The first thing he saw was the large circular bed that occupied most of the room. She laughed seeing his expression. He wondered how it ever got through the door.

'Come in,' she said. 'It's pretty dramatic, yes?' she said. It was more a statement than a question, but he nodded and smiled at her.

The room was a fifteen by fifteen feet square, and other than the enormous bed there was a tiny dresser, a small outdated television from a company that no longer existed.

She had been packing.

'Leaving?' he said.

'Yes, tonight. But I have to check out now.'

He found the hotel phone, and speaking to them in rapid Hindi, he told them that he would pay for an extra night's charge.

'I have convinced them,' he said. 'You can check out later, according to your flight time.'

She screwed her eyebrows at him and said, 'Ankit, you can't do this. I know you must have paid.'

But as she said this, he was moving towards her, and pressing deep against her, he kissed her small, well-defined mouth impatiently.

'Slow down,' she said, whispering by his cheek.

That day Ankit made love for the first time. They made love twice, on the round bed and in the shower, before he was finally spent, and though she was only half-content, she smiled at Ankit, her Indian lover, a lover if only for a brief afternoon. When they dressed, Ankit didn't care about being inconspicuous anymore. He wanted to take her to the best restaurant in Delhi and show her the Delhi he knew. He checked his phone. There were two missed calls from his father. He dismissed it and called up The Oberoi and made a reservation for lunch.

'I love you,' he said to her holding her hips tightly in the stairwell.

She laughed. 'We just met. And you are much too young to know love yet.' She spoke with sad confidence.

When they reached the lobby, he saw his father sitting calmly on the grimy sofa, twirling the ends of his moustache.

The dour receptionist was no longer sitting behind his desk. He stood at attention in a corner examining his feet.

'Let's go,' he said.

'Without the whore,' he added in Hindi.

Annalisa took a step back.

And with the briefest of glances of desperation and desire towards Annalisa, Ankit Kejriwal walked out, shaking with fear, through the coloured glass doors.

They rode the way home in deathly silence. Mishra's every breath trembled with anxiety.

Just as they turned towards the gates of their house the father said, 'Never think I am an idiot.'

'I don't Dad.'

The words had barely escaped Ankit's mouth when he was interrupted with a thundering slap across his left cheek, 'Shut up and listen, you good-for-nothing fool!'

'Your mother and I found this girl with much difficulty. She is from a perfect family and she will make the perfect addition to our family. You are never to meet that whore or any other whore again in this city. You fucking understand me?'

'Yes,' he whispered, his voice barely audible to himself, although he noticed that his father had used the words, 'this city.'

'Now help your mother with the preparations. And put a smile on your face. If you fucked her, at least look happy.' And with that he slammed the door leaving a weeping Ankit with a pale Mishra.

'He called three times on my mobile and demanded to know where you...'

'Shut up!' Ankit screamed. 'Shut up!'

The next evening music boomed around him and the six hundred important guests showered blessings to Ankit and Swati seated on chairs decked with orchids sprayed with psychedelic colours.

When the party finished and a tipsy Swati, overjoyed at the secret experience of drinking alcohol for the first time, went home, when the caterers were eating leftovers in a quiet corner, and the decorators were already stripping the dome of its festive colours exposing the naked scrawny poles, a weary Ankit unfastened the necklaces of emerald and rubies that hung around his brocade kurta.

He removed the kurta that was much too tight around the waist and while removing it he made a small tear on its side. He stood in his bathroom, bare-chested in his churidar, the saffron and vermillion staining his forehead a pale scarlet.

He lit a cigarette and inhaled deeply, thinking of Annalisa, the way her face had contorted with pleasure when he made love to her, the way her eyes had looked up at him when her mouth was on his penis, the way she smelt when he licked the inside of her thighs, her trimmed pubic hair tickling his cheek, her convulsing stomach as she pressed his head against her. He remembered how she had tugged at his gold chain with her mouth, the pendant of Krishna in her mouth and how he had gently prised it from her, removing the chain from his neck for the first time in ten years, placing it on the table beside the bed. He fingered that pendant now, his thoughts alternating between prayer and Annalisa.

Outside, the commotion of disbanding the tenting and decorations sounded just as it had two days earlier and through it all he heard the distinct sound of sobbing. Taken aback, he climbed on the commode and peered through the whirring blades of the exhaust fan.

Mishra was on his knees, sprawled, his hands clutching Ankit's father's legs, his face weeping into his feet. 'Please forgive me,' he kept repeating. 'I have served you for a lifetime!'

'Please forgive me!'

His father kicked Mishra and said, 'You should have thought of that before you took him to that whore. Get out.'

Bachelor

Three months ago in the beginning of autumn, when there was a lull between the rains and the winter, I decided to take advantage of the cool weather to throw what I called The Bachelor's Party. All my friends were married and I was the only bachelor in a group that was constantly trying to match make me with some heiress or princess in the bejewelled Delhi crowd.

I decided on an outdoor party in the garden. The breeze was gentle enough not to make eddies of dust that would spoil the blow-dried hair of the girls and the whiskey of the boys. The tables were laid out with bouquets of white and pink carnations, the food was catered from the Hyatt, and the deejay was accompanied by a young bongo player. I was happy as the evening descended, the gorgeous auburn glow of the low sun made the tips of the hundreds of petals turn rust brown like the burnt edge of cigarette paper. I made my mother take out her finest china, china she had been reserving as gifts to my would-be wife, and although she had not quite given up on a marriage just yet, she could scarcely tell the bread winner of the family what china to use.

I knew it would be a pleasing evening for everyone, and there was always the distinct possibility that we would get perhaps more than just tipsy, and end up dancing on the tops of the tables. I wondered if the girls would dress in sashaying dresses that would skim their cream knees when they danced, the inside shadows of their slender thighs visible, their feet in fashionable stilettos.

But I wanted something more, something different from the usual dinners we all had. The china would be appreciated for no more than a minute by the girls, and scarcely noticed by the men. Buffoons, I thought to myself. The bongo player, obviously a failed musician, passing time playing in wealthy homes would be simply an ornament, a curio with long hair, French beard, sharp features and canvassed shoes. No, he would not be quite enough for my dearest Devika.

Devika Singh, now Devika Mehta, married to my best friend Gaurav Mehta, was the love of my life. She had short hair for a Delhi girl, the curls of her hair, black as night, nuzzled against the white of her neck. It immediately made her stand out from the other girls, all of whom had tresses that reached the middle of their back in dull repetitive hairstyles. She had delightful small moles on her left cheek and under her lip, just faint marks, as if charcoal dots that had been rubbed with butter paper. The hair on her eyebrows were distinct, not just a pencil line of offhand black, but each hair a stroke of different length and depth forming the most unbearable beautiful curve of mathematical purity above eyes that were as innocent as they were large, sparkling like stars, but far brighter than the woeful light of stars that barely made a twinkling through the Delhi smog.

Of all the six couples that were invited, Devika and Gaurav were my favourite, not only because I was in love with his wife but also because I was as much in love with Gaurav. Just as a friend of course, but it was often a joke between us, especially after a whiskey induction, that we were more suited to each other than any woman could ever be. A joke perhaps to him, a joke that was lost on me when Devika would laugh with us, and at us.

Gaurav Mehta had been my best friend since we were toddlers at the Study, a posh school for tots at Golf Links, a school that I hear no longer bodes fascination for the rich and wealthy. After kindergarten, our mothers, in agreeable conspiracy, had given considerable sums of donation that would be considered trivial now and had us admitted at the prestigious St Columba's school for boys, which too, I hear has fallen out of favour, and slipped into a third-class ranking. After our high-school graduation, we stayed back in Delhi while all our friends chose to study management in second grade colleges in the US or UK, a degree they did not need for their family businesses, though a degree from abroad was hallmark enough for Delhi's society for a better education and more importantly, family status and affordability.

Gaurav and I had started work in our respective businesses almost immediately after school, choosing to skip college in favour of joining our fathers and it was telling that well before the rest had graduated, Gaurav and I were already making significant money, and the sums that we had set aside for shopping or gambling in high school seemed paltry now. Yet, it taught us both the value of money; that it was not to be squandered but to be spent wisely and carefully.

When Gaurav and Devika got married, introduced first through his sister, he had a marriage with the right number of ceremonies and tasteful decorations, and although he could have afforded much more glitter and dazzle, he chose to keep everything neatly sophisticated. I appreciated the sensibility and the maturity of my then twenty-five-year-old friend, already a man, far from our school days, but his boyish charm obvious in his playful eyes and striking smile.

It was not that I liked everything about Gaurav. His cheerful and practical optimism often grated on my nerves. I liked to imagine that Devika's sensibility needed a more poetic sensitivity and I could provide her that. And while I could imagine all I liked, it often shattered in my face, when she draped her smooth arm about him, looking at him with loving earnestness when he spoke and I would barely hear him, instead awed at Devika's love for Gaurav, annoyed at my irritation and jealousy, my mind stretched across a plethora of emotions.

What could we play, I thought, pacing the garden. The sun was already behind the trees, the branches scarring the orb of gold, the horizon looking like a mismatched scribble of black and gold lines. The deejay was already setting up his sound system, in conversation with his assistant about cars and an auto show he had seen on BBC. He asked me suddenly, 'So, Sanjiv, what is your favourite car?' while sweeping his arm towards the cars that lined my driveway.

I shrugged. 'Rolls Royce, I guess.'

'Oh.' He said.

And that was it! I thought. We could play a game of questions that one spouse would ask the other to see how well they actually knew each other. This would be absolutely perfect.

A drink for every wrong answer.

Rubbing my hands in practiced glee, I set out to draft the questions. After much scribbling, crossing out, and tearing of paper, I settled on five questions the women would ask the men to bring them to task. I thought of the phrase, 'bring them to task,' and repeatedly rubbed the words in my mouth, enjoying squeezing or expanding the phonetics as I pleased.

What is my shoe size? What is my favourite colour? When did I finish my period? When did I graduate from high school? What is my secret ambition?

While drafting these questions, I fantasised playing the game with Devika, certain that I knew all but one, the question of her period, and God forbid her to be pregnant. Vaguely displeased at my sinister prayer, I made myself the first drink of the evening.

Surely Devika wanted to be a mother soon enough, she was twenty-eight and Gaurav Mehta indisputably would make the perfect father, and well, if she was pregnant, I thought as I finished the drink with an admirable smack of my lips, I would certainly be godfather to the little girl. Of this I was certain; a beauty such as Devika would only have a girl, a cherub of pink cheeks that would bear all resemblance to her perfect mother.

I poured myself a stunningly well-aged Caolilla, flaxen like the horizon, in an old fashioned tumbler that had cost me a hundred pounds, of which I had chosen to buy seven glasses, one for each of the boys, and then I had bought an eighth for Devika, picturing us sitting together in the red loveseat by the electric fireplace, both which had been imported from London, but the picture in my mind was worth more than just money. We would cuddle there in besotted relish, her head on my emollient shoulder, as our tender words would float like butterflies. I thought of all these adjectives and turned them over and over in my mind like an erotic, desperate prayer of longing.

Soon enough, my friends, all married and ready to bear children in a year or so, arrived. Perhaps some of the girls were already pregnant. I curiously observed any signs of not drinking, or lost expressions, perhaps their hands on their cheeks, a faraway look in their eyes bidding adieu to their coquettish girlhood. But tonight as the cool Delhi wind blew about their ruffled tops and chiffon skirts, they gladly accepted margaritas and blush wine, chattering and laughing gaily. Devika and Gaurav looked handsome, her arm was linked through his cream jacket, and although the weather wasn't cool enough, it looked smart and sat well on his tall frame.

She was dressed in a red satin skirt that billowed out from the hip and tapered neatly to her knees. Her top was a white shirt, severely starched, buttoned nearly till the top revealing the spread of her collarbones, and only when she moved her arms, or laughed with her elongated neck could I glimpsed the pink of her bra strap, and was that a little embroidered flower? – I would never know.

After the evening had settled, the starry night admittedly beautiful, the long hair of the bongo player swaying in the breeze and beats, the men pouring their third drinks, and some of the adventurous girls on their second, I announced the game for the evening with a clinking of champagne glasses. As expected, it was met with much amusement from the girls and boos of seasoned exasperation from the boys. I passed around the question cards that had been rushed from my office, neatly printed by my secretary.

Soon enough the game was on, the questions and the answers attracting much hilarity and laughter, but after a few wrong answers, the game took its serious turn, the annoyed expressions of scorn from the girls subduing the preceding mood of merriment. I passed around champagne as the boys screwed up their eyebrows counting away shoe sizes and calculating period intervals.

I observed Devika and Gaurav playing the game by the bar, her arm still resting on him, her eyes in wide enjoyment as she read out the questions. I walked between the tables, jovially commenting and filling drinks, hoping Devika would call me to join them, hoping she would give me a chance to show my mastery, my knowledge about *my* Devika.

And she did, her symphonic voice called my name, 'Sanjiv,' the two syllables distinct from each other as she seemed to draw breath from one to the other. I walked over, scarcely containing my excitement as she asked me to play the game with her.

'The bachelor must play.' She said it to me but looked towards Gaurav, seeking his reassurance.

'By all means,' he said, gentlemanly as ever. 'Devika tells me I have got three right and two wrong but she won't tell me which ones.'

'You have known me five years Sanjiv. Long enough. Let's see how you fare.' She used the word fare, and she said it with affected enjoyment, tilting her head to the side as she said it, the swell of undulating skin and muscle on her neck rousing me considerably.

She asked the questions, even the period one with ready simplicity and gave no indication to the outcome of the answers as I searched her eyes for any clue. Gaurav laughed playfully at every answer vexing my confidence and goading my anxiety.

'You both got three.' She said. 'Two wrong. That is two champagnes gentlemen.'

We both clinked glasses twice and drank the Veuve Cliquot with unabashed challenge and enjoyment.

A duel, I thought.

'I will ask the questions again, till one of you gets one more correct than the other.'

'Sudden death!' exulted Gaurav.

'Indeed, my dear husband. Sudden death indeed.'

She asked the questions again. I noticed we had two answers in common, but that hardly mattered. This time I noticed a little twitch in her eyebrows making the lightest of lines on her forehead, but it was enough for me to sense a hint of displeasure.

I stole the answer concerning her period from Gaurav, quite certain that he would be right, while he stole the shoe size answer from me, knowing that I had bought shoes, several times for Devika in the years.

But her answer was a surprise to both of us. 'Three wrong.'

By this time I could feel the effect of the many whiskeys and the two champagnes that I had drunk in unperturbed confidence.

We downed the three champagnes, drawing deep breaths after each, at the end of which, champagne and whiskey regurgitated back to my mouth.

My head was staggering under the influence of the alcohol, and my feet were tottering. Gaurav looked unsteady too, blinking and shaking his head in rapid succession.

'Let's stop.' said Devika. 'You two boys have had enough for the night.'

'No!' I exclaimed, not willing to bow out of the battle, and Gaurav joined me in my heady chorus.

She questioned us again, and through my drunkenness, I heard her voice – weary and a touch irritable. I couldn't remember my previous answers clearly, and I tried to remember hard and quick as Gaurav spoke, but his inebriated voice was a distant slur, the words incomprehensible to my ears.

When she asked me, I did my best to answer the questions as I had in the first instance, hoping to get three correct answers once again, perhaps four, and if god would have it, all five.

'One right,' said Devika, her voice barely audible as she looked from Gaurav to me.

Shaking her head she said, 'Enough. You two don't know me at all.'

Gaurav dramatically bent down on one knee, and held her right hand, urging me with his free hand to do the same. I bent down as well, two best friends begging forgiveness of the girl we both loved, looking at her with adoring eyes, one perhaps with more longing than the other. Was I proposing to her? Her lips curled in a self-conscious smile as she helped us up, aware of the others watching us, although Gaurav and I were too drunk to notice or care.

We both had four glasses each, much to Devika's dismay and protests that sounded weak and distant. This time we chugged with ready gusto and untidy abandonment, the champagne spilling, from chin to shirt.

'Last time. And that's it. And you better do better Gaurav.' She said, looking at Gaurav accusatorily. Then she turned to me, 'I don't mean you should do worse than him though,' pointing towards him like he was an object. She spoke to me softly, her words more kind towards me than him, and with that my drunken stupor brightened a bit.

Once again, she asked us the questions. This time her face seemed calm, perhaps Gaurav had indeed got the answers right, and when she asked me, I did my best to remember his answers.

'I think I'll join the girls,' she said pointing to the table where all the girls were playing the same game with each other.

'What's the outcome this time darling?' said Gaurav in a voice that stumbled with every word, as syllable pushed against syllable with slurring insensibility.

'Not one right, dear gentlemen. Not one.' Her words shook ever so slightly, her heart was upset, her steps towards the tables short and quick.

Gaurav and I paused. Then he draped his arm around my shoulder, his laughter easily betraying the rotten feeling of his shaken confidence. I smiled at this, but my insides burned like simmering charcoal as we turned to the bar and ordered more champagne.

The Company

Every year Mr Bhatnagar wore his winter woollens from 15 November until 15 February. No matter whether it got hot or cold before or after those dates, Mr Bhatanagar only wore the sweaters for exactly those three months.

Mr Bhatanagar had worked for the accounts department at Chopra Real Estate for twenty-seven years and although he had never been a creative accountant, he was thorough and his desk was always tidy. This was remarkable in itself in a business that was tediously cumbersome with innumerable government regulations that meant mountains of paperwork and years of crumbling files in an accounts department that heaved with stress and anxiety.

The tax returns had to be filed thrice a year, the sales tax and service tax had to be calculated and paid before the fifth of every month, countless forms and regulatory paperwork had to be filled in, exchanged, and submitted between hundreds of suppliers, contractors, clients and government agencies.

It was Mr Bhatnagar's job to oversee the twenty-people accounts department and report to Aman Chopra, the owner of the company. Aman's father had started the company but at his passing two years earlier, Aman had emerged from his shadow to be an earnest if not an astute businessman with the acumen of his father.

When Aman took over the business, it was assumed that he would take over his father's office space too – a mahogany panelled enclosure of Chesterfields and an elaborately carved desk, an excellent and expensive imitation of nineteenth-century French design. Aman chose to leave his father's office as is, instead building adjacent to it a glass enclosure with a workstation and a small table for meetings. The door to his cabin was always open; the blinds never drawn. The way it is everywhere in the world, he noted. Some of the older employees, including Mr Bhatnagar, had requested him to take over his father's room, but he had politely refused.

Although their young boss wasn't conventional and not as traditional or pious as they would have liked, he did always entered his father's office every morning to garland his grandfather's and father's photographs with fresh flowers and burn jasmine infused incense.

Over the past two years, the changes Aman had introduced with hesitant boldness were not always welcome, indeed some decisions were met with outright dismay and resentment, but many of the employees grudgingly respected the decisions that clearly had the makings of an overhaul the thirty- year-old business needed.

In Mr Bhatnagar's twenty-eighth year, Diwali came sooner than usual, this time on 15 October, nearly three weeks earlier than most years. And with an early Diwali, the winter came early too. Although it was not as cold as some of the Octobers Mr Bhatanagar had witnessed, it was cold enough to wear a sweater.

When on 23 October Mr Bhatnagar came to office, wearing a green sweater that some had seen him wear since his first winter at Chopra Real Estate, he was met with surprise and amusement. Even the peons shyly smiled as he made his way to his workstation, one of the larger workstations with two visitor chairs. When Aman came to work, he too screwed his eyebrows at the appearance of the too-familiar green sweater well before its appointed time. After setting down his laptop in his cabin, garlanding the two photographs and burning the incense, he walked out and took a seat opposite Mr Bhatnagar.

'All okay, Mr Bhatnagar?' he said.

'Sir, you always talk about change. I thought it was time for change. It is cold, so I wore the sweater,' Mr Bhatnagar said with a pleased smile.

Aman laughed. 'Some changes aren't necessary, Mr Bhatnagar.'

'Thank you, sir. But it is cold. And one shouldn't hang on to silly superstitions.' He smiled at Aman kindly like a father would.

Aman was grateful for the smile and also secretly pleased that Mr Bhatnagar had done away with his tradition, something he always found silly even as a school boy when his father would tell him about his work during the Sunday walks they took after visiting the Hanuman temple. He would listen wide-eyed as his father pointed out the houses they had built and sold – three-storey structures with lavishly-appointed apartments on each floor.

They were revolutionizing the way the average well-off Delhiite lived, his father told him. He would point out to Aman plot sizes and explain their price points. He would tell him about terrace rights and gardens. He showed him how the model worked profitably, keeping the average apartment cost far lower than a plot price yet affording the buyer a living in the heart of South Delhi. He told him with a distinct smacking of the lips how the sum of the parts, the apartments, was greater than the whole, the plot.

Aman would listen proudly and on the school bus he would point out the dozens of homes and apartments that his father had built, some even occupied by his friends. Now twenty years later as he took some of the same familiar route to his office, he looked at those homes, many of them since refurbished by Chopra Real Estate and he smacked his lips like his father and tears brimmed from his eyes that always looked earnestly sad.

Aman had started working immediately after school, choosing to study in Delhi University through correspondence, shunning the idea of studying abroad, unlike most of his friends. His sincere disposition endeared him to everyone, even the shrewd brokers they did business with. He dutifully went about his work, always listening to his father's advice, and although not entirely content within the constraints his father had set, he never disobeyed him. He timidly gave ideas and suggestions at the weekly meetings in which he was always seated to his father's right and whenever any of them were accepted he felt deeply grateful and obliged to a father he considered God.

Three years after joining the business, standing at the pyre of his father, pouring ghee into the crackling flames, his eyes stinging as much from smoke as sorrow, he was aware that over a hundred employees stood there amidst a thousand people, and the importance of the moment through the mottled, desperate grief was not lost on him. He saw his mother sobbing into the arms of his sister. He saw his father's brother whom he had not seen in years. He saw relatives who had flown from Bombay and Calcutta, and he saw his friends whose fathers were still alive standing alongside them.

He saw bankers and clients and wondered if their foreheads were creased with genuine grief or with worry about their investments and business.

Thirteen days after the cremation, and after the immersion of the ashes and the ceremonies, he called on his bankers and clients. With his senior colleagues, including Mr Bhatnagar, he held short but convincing meetings about their ability to keep commitments. Clients and bankers alike had been outwardly loyal and bowed out of the office with much show of respect and promises of resolute and lifelong support.

In the two years since his father's death, Aman had been cautious, containing and consolidating their investments and positions. It was this that was much appreciated within the company that thought him to have too many grandiose plans too soon.

Although many had jeered and mocked at Mr Bhatnagar's wearing his sweater three weeks too soon, and even as the entire office was a blotching of bright sweaters in the early winter, a quiet change ensued through the company. At first it was imperceptible and marked with jokes and amusement.

Mr Anand, the main purchase officer of the business had a habit of smoking beedis at least three times a day: after lunch, at tea and before the close of the day. Although he could easily afford cigarettes, it was beedi he was addicted to, and his cubicle stank of the bitter smell.

'I will give up smoking,' he declared one day at lunch. This was met with incredulity and scepticism from all, including Aman who bemusedly listened to the hoots and boos.

But two weeks went by and Mr Anand had not smoked a single beedi. Mr Anand, his chest even more puffed than usual, waxed eloquent on the benefits of yoga, meditation and exercise. These were the secret to his willpower, he explained during the twenty-minute afternoon walk he took with his colleagues after lunch in the busy by-lanes of Panchsheel.

During one of these walks, urged by the claims of Mr Anand, they decided to make use of the huge terrace above their office which was empty barring a couple of water tanks. They came to Aman with the idea of buying a table-tennis table and setting up a small badminton court for their afternoon leisure activity. A yoga teacher was also appointed to come on alternate days. Aman readily agreed to these new developments, thrilled at their initiative.

Three days later, the terrace tiles were scarred with the white lines of a badminton court. The table-tennis table and yoga mats occupied one corner of the expansive terrace.

The mood at the office was cheerful and abounded with enthusiasm for the first time since his father's death.

The excitement and spirit was the perfect time for Aman to present them with new ideas. The Delhi real estate market was booming and it was an opportune time for their company to make significant forays.

At the end of November, when Delhi was shivering with a piercingly cold winter, he held a series of meetings, for the first time in his father's office, with his most-trusted employees. Although he did not take his father's chair to the disappointment of his colleagues, they were quickly absorbed in Aman's determined tone convincing them of investing in large plots of land in the satellite towns of Noida, Greater Noida and Gurgaon.

'We are falling behind,' he said. 'Competitors we would have not thought worthy are giving full-page advertisements in national papers.' He showed them the past weeks' newspapers, demonstrating his point. They had to move past the south Delhi market and enter mass housing and commercial developments of offices and malls. He tapped his fist against his palm to make his point. It was time for Chopra Real Estate to escalate to the next level.

His colleagues were excited with these prospects, indeed there had been murmurs within that they were holding back. Their bank balances were burgeoning, the team was experienced, and it was the right moment to strike the market. Exactly two months after Mr Bhatnagar had broken tradition, channelling a domino effect of change throughout the company, Chopra Real Estate came out with its first full-page advertisement in all the national dailies announcing their forays into Noida and Gurgaon with a hundred acres of development in the pipeline.

On New Year's Eve, Aman threw a massive party at Taj Palace Hotel, booking the largest banquet hall for 2,000 people. A beaming Aman, resplendent in a black Nehru suit, a carnation in his buttonhole greeted guests at the entrance. Assisted by Mr Bhatnagar at the entrance, he shook hands with bureaucrats, ministers, government officials, clients, bankers, financiers, investors, brokers, and a smattering of close friends who had not left Delhi for Goa or Koh Samui.

Two days after New Years, on a morning when the fog clung closely to the disfigured Delhi roads, a still-tired and slightly hung-over Aman lit incense at the photographs, praying through closed sleepy eyes for a prosperous year ahead. Just as he opened the door of his father's office, he saw a frightened Mr Bhatnagar.

'Sir, we have men from the income-tax department for a survey,' Mr Bhatnagar said in a terrified voice that both alarmed and irritated him.

Aman raised his eyebrows at Mr Bhatnagar and in a low voice asked him, 'How many have come?'

'Seven.'

'Home?'

'Not yet. Your mother has been informed.'

'Where are they?'

And just as he said this, there appeared two men, one large and heavyset, his mehandi-streaked hair barely covering his bald patch, the other gaunt, the skin on his face pulled against sharp cheekbones, his hair startlingly white. It was almost comic, Aman thought as he shook hands with them.

'Hello sir. Happy New Year,' said the larger man, his smile revealing tobacco-stained teeth. The hand Aman shook was fat and damp.

'Happy New Year, sir. What can we do for you?' Aman asked genially, but with a slight tremble in his voice evident.

'Sir, the usual. Nothing much. We don't want to bother you at all. Just a routine check of the books.' He patted down his mehandi hair looking at the other man who was eyeing the desk greedily.

'Everything is up-to-date at our office sir,' said Aman, looking towards Mr Bhatnagar for reassurance who nodded vigorously in agreement.

'We paid good taxes last year,' said Mr Bhatnagar. 'Almost ten crore.'

'Sir, this is just routine. Don't worry. If all is in order, what's the problem? The finance ministry is conducting a survey in all real-estate companies. Twenty, simultaneously today.' He said it in a triumphant voice.

With that and without asking for permission they walked into his father's office. Aman motioned Mr Bhatnagar to go in. He wanted to see for himself what was happening in the main office area.

The other four men and one woman were already busying themselves around several workstations, and all his employees had worried, anxious expressions. One of them was sitting at

Mr Anand's computer sipping the steaming tea that was being passed around by frightened peons. Mr Anand was leaning over the man's shoulder, his voice sounding decidedly gruff and annoyed.

When he saw Aman, he strode quickly towards him and said, 'Don't worry sir. We'll have them out of here in no time.' He said it confidently, and Aman was glad to accept the assurance, in contrast to the nervous Mr Bhatnagar.

He knew it would not be over quickly. Surveys could take days. He shivered at the thought. He walked back into his father's office, crossing his glass cabin where the woman was thumbing through his files, licking her index finger each time she turned a page. She looked at him, her expression blank, her purple lipstick untidily smeared across her wide lips, her sari tight around her belly, the short grey sweater bursting at the buttonholes, failing to cover the stretch-mark-streaked stomach that clumsily tumbled between the sari and the sweater.

He walked back to his father's office and immediately felt sickened at the sight of the two men lounging on the green chesterfields, holding tea cups with both hands, commenting on how cold the weather was. Unusually cold, they said looking at him. Mr Bhatnagar nodded in ready agreement, his green sweater much too pale, and much too weathered.

'Let's get this over with quickly sir,' said Aman.

'Calm down boy,' said the thin man sharply in a scratchy voice that made the back of Aman's legs quiver with fear and loathing. 'These things take time. You should know this.'

He called his mother and sister to reassure them, but also longing to hear the much needed sympathetic love in their voices. He made several calls to influential friends. They all promised to help. They spoke to him in concerned tones, ringed with the touch of excitement that drama brings.

He knew he was not calling as much for help as for empathy, and he could almost see their nodding heads as nearly all affirmed that this had happened to their business too. They shared how much bribe would work. Depends on your turnover and past profits, they said in voices that tried to fruitlessly mask their inquisitiveness. In these conversations he too became a part of the club of businessmen for whom this was to be expected, almost routine, a coming of age, and to be handled with cool aplomb.

Aman, Mr Bhatnagar, and Mr Anand pleaded and prayed with the thin man who was the operations head. They unsuccessfully told him that their books were clean and each time his response was as hackneyed as their pleadings. 'Declare fifteen crore as tax arrears and we can close this quickly.' He said it with a yawn, waggling his head side to side.

Mr Bhatnagar protested, but his voice was meek. Hours of interrogation turned Mr Anand's aggressive tone exhausted and bitterly submissive.

'Bhanagar sahib, you're old and experienced. Your hair is white with wisdom. Not like this young man with his fire-hot blood. How many papers and scribbles will you explain? Come on, declare and we can end this right now.' The thin man twirled a pen towards Mr Bhatnagar as if offering a bone to a dog.

Aman was exhausted. It had been thirty hours. Even though it was past noon, Delhi outside could hardly be heard, and the fog was thicker than ever before. The woman was questioning him in a tone that was weary but unconcerned with the hours and her own tiredness, her authority giving her an aura of gloating satisfaction. Her lips interrogated and barked, for explaining numbers and figures that he had scribbled on sheets of paper, numbers that were just musings and meant nothing. He broke down, tears streamed from his reddened eyes and he clasped his hands together in fervent prayer and begged her to leave him alone, begged her to let him sleep.

The office of Chopra Real Estate became silent, as they all watched and heard their boss weep into his hands. Mr Anand strode in and laid a gentle hand on Aman's head. But Aman was already asleep; his head between his arms, his body slouched over troubled dreams.

When he woke an hour later, he saw his fatigued colleagues shuffling from one file cabinet to the other, their eyes glassed over, the tax officials with their feet propped on workstations and snapping fingers for tea and snacks. The air was gloomy and stale with smoke from the countless cigarettes, nearly as thick as the fog outside.

A clouded Delhi, thought Aman resentfully. The woman was asleep, her plump calloused feet spread out on a chair, the frayed ends of a grimy petticoat visible, her open mouth no longer purple as she snored vulgarly.

He walked around the office. The floor was strewn with papers, files, packets of chips and biscuits. The urinals and washbasins in the bathroom were stained red with the spit of gutkha.

Several dozen files were tied with thin white rope. Their knots were sealed with wax, the stamp bore the words, 'Income Tax Deptt'. Some of the computers were boxed into cartons, their fate too sealed with stamped red wax.

Inside his father's office, the man with the mehandi hair snored peacefully, his hands comfortably interlaced across his chest, his broad body snuggled in the thick green leather of the Chesterfield, his dirty sneakers crossed over the armrest. Mr Bhatnagar and the thin man appeared in a low-voiced discussion and on seeing Aman, Mr Bhatnagar immediately got up and led Aman outside.

'They are willing to settle,' he said.

'How much?' asked Aman, aware that both their breaths stank with stale morning breath.

'They want ten lacs, you know...'

Aman nodded impatiently.

'And they want us to declare five crore of additional profits, nothing less.' When he spoke his eyes were downcast, and Aman felt pity for this man who had served his father, his company, for the last twenty-seven years. He held Mr Bhatnagar by his left shoulder and told him he supported him in whatever he decided. They both knew that the tax officials could find many faults in the books, faults that could cost them much more if they held to their stance of stubborn innocence. It was futile.

The money was arranged and it came in a small bag that advertised a tailoring shop not too far from their office. The price of freedom, thought Aman.

In the end when the officials left after forty hours, when morning was just peeking through a Delhi that huddled against the intense cold, the office of Chopra Real Estate heaved a sigh of exhausted relief. Aman shook the hands of all his employees and thanked them uncomfortably for their loyalty and support.

In the next few weeks, business returned to normal at Chopra Real Estate, but the employees had lost their enthusiasm, their new energy. The badminton net sagged and the table-tennis table and yoga mats were covered in splotches of bird shit. The employees returned to their walks amidst fumes and traffic. Mr Anand started smoking again, the smell of beedis clung on him defiantly. Along with the ten lakh, the boxed computers and files, the men from the government had tied the heart of the company in a deep knot and poured hot wax on their new dreams.

That year the winter in Delhi was unyielding and obstinate. In the middle of February when the air was still chilly, Mr Bhatnagar came shivering to Aman's cabin in a familiar blue shirt that had discoloured entirely after so many years.

'Everyone wants you to shift to your father's room Aman sir.'

He continued, 'They believe, and so do I, that it is bad luck for you to sit in this glass room, and especially under a beam,' he pointed at the ceiling. 'We have been through bad luck. The evil eye is upon us.'

He hesitated before continuing, 'Mr Chopra's *aatma* will not rest peacefully until his room is occupied by the rightful owner. And that is you.'

Aman looked at Mr Bhatnagar thoughtfully, hearing his trembling words squelching against each other. He pressed the bell for the peon.

'Ram,' he said commandingly, 'pack my stuff and shift it to bade sahab's room.'

In a grateful but shivering voice, Mr Bhatnagar said, 'Thank you Aman. Thank you.'

'It's cold Mr Bhatnagar, it's still very cold.'

Mr Bhatnagar smiled, 'Sir, some changes aren't necessary.'

Dior

When Payal Seth heard that she had given birth to a healthy baby boy, she was delighted at the news, relieved that it was a boy. Through the blur of the retreating anaesthesia, she knew her husband, Kapil Seth, would have been outwardly pleased had it been a girl, but at least now both Kapil and her mother-in-law would swell with genuine satisfaction.

These were her first thoughts and when she cradled the baby against her breast, she looked at the crinkly folds of skin around the closed eyes of her infant and remembered the night he was conceived.

It was a Saturday night towards the end of May, and the night had been unusually cool for that time of the year. A grateful Delhi had swamped the lawns of India Gate, enjoying the respite in the weather.

Kapil and Payal were to go out that night to celebrate a friend's thirty-fifth birthday. The same morning, Kapil had complained loudly that it would be much too hot and what was his friend thinking of, having an outdoor party. Payal shook her head as she heard these rants. He must have noticed because he looked at her angrily and said, 'What, what!'

'Calm down, *jaan*. It's not that hot. Remember, last night you woke me up to raise the temperature?' She said it almost playfully, because he had nudged her again and again with his erection, with closed eyes and a cranky mouthful of mumbled words. She had found the extraordinary manner of request amusing. At least it's of some use, she thought with a hint of derision.

He gruffly returned to his breakfast, stabbing at the centre of the yolk in the fried egg, the yellow staining the white thoroughly. He was five foot ten, a medium built man with large arms and a chest to show that he bore weights regularly to keep them as hard as stone. His stomach wasn't quite as hard or flat and in fact protruded beyond his belt when he sat, a fact that he hated, so he sat as little as possible and when he did, he sat with his back straight, and his stomach tucked in as tightly as he could without contorting his face into comical expressions.

'Maya!' he yelled.

'What jaan?' answered Payal instead. 'She's probably packing your food. What do you want?' Her tone was sweet, her eyes eager to please her husband.

'I am late for work. I don't want lunch today.'

'It will be ready in a minute Kapil. You have to have lunch.'

'I don't want it.' And with that he stood up, the remains of the fried egg still bleeding its contents on a cream coloured plate decorated with gold patterns on its fringe.

The maid, Maya, rushed after him, and even as she reached the slammed door of the black Honda SUV, he waved impatiently at the chauffeur to drive. Maya stood helplessly at the doorway, easy tears welling up in her eyes as Payal patted her oiled hair and told her gently not to worry.

That evening when Kapil came back from work, he hungrily ate a solitary apple and washed it down with two cups of black coffee. Payal watched her husband, knowing well not to say anything. She knew he was starving himself to lose a quick kilo. He always did that before a big party.

'You are right,' he said. 'The weather isn't bad at all. Lucky bastard, that Mohit. If it was as hot as it has been the party would have been a total fucking flop.'

He looked at his wife for acquiescence, and she nodded her agreement, barely hearing the words, worrying instead about what she would wear. It would be the last of the big parties before Delhi disappeared to Europe or New York for the holidays, and even though it was summer, the social circuit had been unusually busy. So she had to be careful not to repeat an outfit that anyone would remember from a recent occasion.

She searched her wardrobe as Kapil showered and by the time he had stepped out she had laid three dresses on the bed.

'What do you think?' she asked. He eyed them contemptuously. 'Do you fit well into them? You know...' And as he said that, he dug playfully into her tummy.

'It's just a little baby fat,' said Payal, her voice evidently hurt, thinking of the skinny girls that pouted from the covers of GQ and Esquire that were strewn around the commode in their bathroom.

'I'll wear the black one. You like that as well,' she pleaded.

'Didn't you wear that recently?'

'That was two months ago. No one will remember. It's fine.'

He shrugged as he stood naked in their wardrobe area; naked while sifting through the countless colours of shirts that made the inside of his wardrobe look like it had all the colours of a spring garden in full bloom. He wore his favourite dark blue jeans and flexed his chest and biceps repeatedly, eyeing himself in the full length mirror. But his eyes kept wandering to his stomach and clutched at it in wanting.

'Which shirt?' he said holding up a brown Gucci and a white Dolce and Gabbana.

She knew his preference was the Gucci shirt because it was not as tight fitting as the other one. But she also knew she had to give delicate reasoning. If she resolutely gave her opinion about the Gucci shirt, she knew Kapil would jump at her and accuse her of believing that he didn't fit well in the other one.

Feeling a headache creep up at these superfluous thoughts she said thoughtfully, 'Well the D&G looks beautiful on you jaan, but it's a big party and someone stupid is bound to spill wine.'

'You are right!' he said jubilantly. 'Besides, the brown one fits me a bit better.' He added, 'My arms look much better in it.'

With a sigh Payal stepped into the shower, looking at her naked body in the mirror. What isn't attractive about me, she wondered as she looked at her oval face, her large brown eyes, the wet eyelashes that clung together in large spikes, her full mouth of natural pinkness. She looked over her elegant shoulder at her lush hair that formed a perfect shape of flowing waves.

'Come on baby!' shouted Kapil even though they both knew that she would still be ready before him.

She slipped into the black dress, her hair wet, her thighs still moist. It was a perfect little black dress, and at what a bargain, she thought gratefully. It had a deep neck, elegantly narrow, and the dancing cleavage of her generous breasts was just visible.

She blowdried her hair into perfect luscious locks, perfumed her wrists, dabbed her neck, glossed her lips, and stood ready before Kapil glancing dubiously at his watch box.

'I need a new watch.' Payal mouthed these words to herself and no sooner than she had, she heard Kapil mutter in irritation, 'I need a new watch.'

'Wear the new Cartier jaan. It's very smart.'

'It's got a black strap,' he snapped. 'It doesn't quite go with this, does it?' gesturing at his brown shoes, belt and shirt.

'No one will notice Kapil. Besides it is a beautiful watch.'

'What kind of shoes are you wearing?' he said strapping on the Cartier.

She looked at him questioningly.

'Those,' he said pointing at her shoes, 'are too worn out. Wear the new Dior ones we got last weekend.'

'Aren't they too patent? Much too glossy to go with this dress?' she said.

'No one will notice Payal. Besides they are beautiful shoes,' he said mockingly, uneasily content to mirror her words.

The drive to the party was forty-five minutes away from their Punjabi Bagh residence. Kapil repeatedly changed songs on the iPod, barely hearing any one for one minute, humming tunes under his breath, sipping whiskey from an old-fashioned cut glass. He swirled it, enjoying the reflected lights of Delhi traffic skipping through its golden colours. Payal too sipped whiskey, not because she enjoyed it but because she wanted to get a little drunk. The only way I'll get through yet another party, she thought.

There were flyover constructions all over Ring Road till the Dhaula Kuan intersection and the sound of heavy machinery and the laughter of exhausted workers in yellow helmets wafted in the car that weaved slowly through the impatient honking traffic making its way around traffic cones and bright diversion boards. At Dhaula Kuan, they took National Highway 8, and the traffic sped up across four lanes, but Delhi traffic was unaccustomed to such magnanimity, and the traffic was still untidily chaotic.

'Fucking city,' said Kapil changing songs once again.

Payal bristled at Kapil's usual rant, but knowing better than to start yet another pointless argument, she downed her whiskey in a gulp. Kapil was snapping his fingers, bobbing his head at some song and he patted Payal's knee, encouraging her. She smiled at him, nodding back, but not joining in, partly because she knew this was all the dancing she would get from him for the night, and partly because she was too shy to do so, her eyes occasionally catching the eye of the driver in the rear-view mirror. He had been with Payal since she was ten years old, and he was a part of the dowry as Kapil liked to joke, a joke she found highly tasteless and especially as it was oft-repeated in front of Jaan Singh as if he didn't understand even that bit of English.

They crossed the international airport on their right and she looked appreciatively as Singapore Airlines made its landing approach, the roar of its engines drowning the hackneyed dance music, the streaking yellow light from its windows looking hauntingly beautiful. She wondered what she would feel about India if she were a visiting foreigner. Would she think it was Incredible !ndia? Yes, she thought proudly. Yes, she would.

They turned left at the Westend Greens farmhouse complex, the private guards at the entrance saluting smartly at the many cars that were undoubtedly pouring in for the party.

'Just in time,' said Kapil appreciatively. It was eleven thirty, the moon was full and beaming, the sky clear and cool.

The commotion outside the farmhouse was strangely comforting, thought Payal. Guards whistled cars forward, waving their arms about energetically as guests in their glamorous outfits greeted each other like showy automatons with hugs and kisses. Payal adjusted her neckline self-consciously, aware of the leering stares of the valet drivers in their white outfits and brassy buttons.

The men inside are no better, she thought.

Kapil was already walking ahead, rolling back his shirt sleeves as if entering a fight not a party, his broad shoulders arched back, his chin decidedly pointing upwards. The driveway was long, lined with carved lanterns of Dholpur that cast intricate elongated shadows on the cobbled granite, in the gaps of which Payal's heels kept getting stuck and chafed.

The throbbing bass was easily heard before she saw the fuchsia pink tenting of the party in the vast garden. Crystals as big as her hand tumbled irregularly down the sides of the huge tent, but in the next instant it was obvious that it spelt out the name of the host whose birthday it was – Mohit.

No doubt he would insist that it was his wife's idea, Payal thought. No doubt he would repeat that many times and especially when he got drunk, splattering spit and bad breath with every word.

Kapil was already a distant speck, she could see him high-fiving or hugging the men and air-kissing the women with discerning delight, taking time with the prettier ones, planting his lips full on each cheek as he held them about their ivory shoulders, the tips of their breasts just grazing his puffed chest. The popularity of her husband, though attractive, also repulsed her. She couldn't decide what she felt for him that night. She took a sharp intake of breath and braced herself for another party night.

The lawn was carpeted. Thank god, she thought. At least her heels won't sink in the grass. The dance floor was still quite empty and the party pressed itself against the bar, rows of single malts and exotic vodkas lining the back counter of stained glass. Everyone shouted proprietarily at the familiar bartenders dressed in sharp tuxedos. Drinks were quickly swirled and served, the occasional sound of a champagne pop bringing cheer and laughter amidst rouged cheeks and gelled hair.

Payal met all whom she knew with perfunctory ease and grace, her neckline openly complimented and commented on, teasingly and jealously by the girls, and eyed lustily in split second glances by the men who kissed her cheeks in appreciative gesture. A few drinks and it would not just be split second nervous glances, she thought. Some would put their arms about her shoulders and let their greedy hands hang limply, hungry for the tips of their fingers to touch the swell of her breasts. Pathetic, she thought, making her way to the bar.

The party was soon swarming, groups of friends swayed amidst gossip and laughter, the booming music played English and Hindi songs, and the deejay tried to play to everyone's taste, switching from 80s to R&B, old Hindi mixed with new beats and to the occasional hip-hop. Payal at the bar caught fleeting glimpses of her husband who skipped from group to group making his way through the crowd and even though she could not hear him, she could imagine his throaty laughter and his easy words.

How they had fallen in love, she wondered. The single malt made her heart beat faster. Four years ago, they had been the golden couple, the toast of friends and family, the couple everyone admired openly and envied secretly. Was she too young then at twenty-two? Had he changed? Had they both changed?

She shook these questions from her mind as she joined her girlfriends at the bar. She decided to get further drunk. She shot down three tequila shots in a row amidst hoots of encouragement when she felt a pat in the middle of her back.

'Easy Payal,' she heard words that sounded comfortingly familiar, a mix of amusement and concern about them.

'Rohit!' she cried flinging her arms about his neck hugging him close, closer than she normally would.

Rohit Mishra was Kapil Seth's closest friend. Kapil and Rohit had known each other all their lives. She held him by the shoulders and eyed him critically and lovingly, letting her hands drop to his chest. His shirt was untucked and a little too large for him. His hair was dishevelled and his stubble at least a week old. His eyes shone with clarity and humour, his lips turned in a ready, easy smile.

'Have you met Kapil?' Payal asked, her voice slurring slightly.

'Of course,' he said. 'It's you I haven't seen in ages. Your husband and I keep meeting for lunch from work.'

'oh, now I know why he doesn't carry his lunch these days,' she exclaimed.

'He hardly eats. I eat his food as well,' he said, approvingly tapping at his stomach. They both laughed.

'Come, let's dance,' said Payal cheerfully.

The coloured acrylic of the dance floor was lit from the underside and everyone drunk, messy, and aflame, danced in a big heave. Payal and Rohit squeezed on through a corner. They could barely move, mashing against the many people, their drunken jives and bizarre moves. Kapil was dancing too, and as if with the whole floor, as he moved from group to group rocking his shoulders in drunken eagerness. Payal felt sickened with his usual performance.

She and Rohit could barely dance in the jostling crowd, instead they held each other closely, their backs against the swirling mass of people, her arms about his neck, his on her waist. She was happily indifferent, comfortable in his embrace, in hands that felt confident and in control. The look in his eyes was mischievously familiar, the endless depth behind them as riveting as heartbreaking. She moved her waist closer, so that their thighs touched every few beats. The pressure of his hands on her waist tightened slightly, and in the comfortable movement of their bodies, Payal thought how wonderful it would be with this very different and charming man.

'Let's get a little air,' she pleaded, aware of her clichéd words, but it didn't matter. They ducked through an opening in the tent by the dance floor. Rohit went through first, and he held the tent back as Payal came through, deliberately not covering her neckline, allowing him to see her full cleavage, and when she looked at him, his eyes were bereft of their usual clarity and humour, instead arousal filling them, like wine splashing in a clear glass.

'I need to use a bathroom,' she said. 'But I don't want to use those,' she pointed at the rows of rented cubicles.

He motioned towards the house. 'Let's go inside.'

They walked into the main house. The servant smiled at Rohit and opened the door. Everyone likes Rohit, she thought.

In the hall, a massive chandelier cascaded down in spirals and twists, from a silver-leaf ceiling and a giant granite Buddha perched in the centre of the indoor lily pond. Orchids and roses filled the crystal vases that decorated the several consoles and credenzas that lined walls of pink patterned wallpaper. Hideous, she thought.

'Hideous,' said Rohit as though reading her mind, opening a door of oak veneer revealing a guest room.

'How come you have access inside this house?' she asked.

'I know Mohit very well. Kapil knows him just as well too. The three of us meet often.'

'Oh. He never tells me these things.'

He shrugged. 'No big deal. It's usually a work lunch to grab a bite and a few laughs.'

'You mean escaping work lunch,' said Payal, as she shut the bathroom door to his laughing expression.

She turned the tap on fully so he couldn't hear her pee. When she was done, she opened the door. Her face pressed close to the mirror, she applied fresh make up. She glossed her lips, rouged her cheeks and dabbed perfume from a miniature bottle. She could see Rohit's reflection and she smiled at him between her actions.

'You don't need it Payal,' he said pointing at the various bottles in her purse. 'You are already incomparably beautiful.'

She laughed, her cheeks reddening naturally. 'Thank you Rohit.'

'You haven't said that to me in years,' she said in a tone mockingly accusatory.

'Doesn't mean I never say it.'

'Thank you Rohit.' This time her voice was sincere and her tone quiet.

And no sooner had she said the words, she found herself turned around by his hands on her waist. In his arms they looked at each other, each suspenseful and aware, each searching in the other's eyes. Payal closed her eyes, her eyelashes knitted together, and they kissed, their mouths open, their lips embracing in hungry passion. They kissed for as long as time could afford them to.

They heard voices in the hallway. Payal rushed inside the bathroom. Rohit smoothed his unkempt hair and walked outside the guest room. It was Mohit and Kapil with some friends. All of them were drunkenly hollering, holding champagne glasses toasting towards the Buddha statue.

'Hey Rohit!' shouted Kapil. 'Have you seen a girl called Payal? Did she get lost?' he snickered.

'She's in the bathroom,' said Rohit calmly.

Payal walked out, her hair perfect, her face beautifully made up and as Rohit and she stood by each other looking at the drunken group, both could smell the flavour of love between them.

'Hey baby!' Kapil hollered. 'Let's go home! Let's make some love baby!'

Dismayed and embarrassed at his ludicrous words, as much for herself as for Rohit, she whispered, 'Let's go jaan. Let's go. It is late.'

Much to her surprise, Kapil did not pass out in the car but played the iPod on full volume, prompting Jaan Singh to throw more than a casual glance at the pretty woman in the rear-view mirror, a little girl to him. She looked sad as she watched the lonely Ring Road, the heavy machinery with its motionless arms, the yellow helmets scattered about on iron rods like homage to construction workers, the cat's eye reflectors menacingly bright and yellow against the tar of the newly built roads.

At home, he climbed onto her impatiently, not bothering to remove her dress or his shirt, pushing himself in her and after the repeated motion of sex, he fell asleep on top of her just as soon as he came in exhaustion.

A few days later she took the pregnancy test and the result was positive. When she told Kapil that she was pregnant, he jumped up and much to her grateful surprise he was delighted at the news. He immediately wore his track pants and without asking her opinion, rushed to the other wing of the house to tell his parents. She was glad that he was happy.

What she had done with Rohit was redeemed, she thought, although as she rubbed her stomach, her thoughts were only with Rohit, the press of his lips, the soft sounds of affection he made.

Nine months and ten days later after a full-term pregnancy, her hand was on her stitches, the remembrance of that night bringing a secret smile to her weary lips. In the adjacent room, she could hear Kapil bickering about the quality of service at the hospital, and through the cacophony of pitched voices, she heard Rohit.

'No, no, please Kapil. She must be resting. Tell her I came. Love to the baby. Congratulations.'

Diwali

I was surprised I was attracted to her. She did not have a beautiful face. Her nose was imperfect, her forehead much too small and her lips thin. But she had neat, sparkling teeth, blazing clear eyes, a ring of humour around her iris, a firm jawline, straight, unfussed hair.

We were introduced on Diwali at the annual party thrown by Gaurav Gupta. Gaurav Gupta's popularity ebbed with Diwali and flowed away just as Diwali ended. I could see him wandering through the colossal party, his knuckles white, holding a Scotch, his face red and ruddy as he hugged and kissed those who would surely forget him tomorrow.

It was mid October, the dredges of summer clung to the air, winter waited in the wings.

I learnt she was married when our conversation was interrupted by a man much older than her, bald, bearded, short, green eyed, and in an obviously expensive cream leather jacket. He whispered into her ear and walked on, without an apology or introduction.

'Sorry, that was my husband,' she said apologetically, her eyes immediately reading the quizzical look in mine.

'You're married,' I said. 'Yes, three years. And you?' I laughed. 'I was.' 'Oh.' 'It's fine.' I clarified. 'More than fine. But perhaps you wouldn't like to talk to me now?' I jeered. Immediately I regretted my condescension. She looked at me scornfully, her eyebrows rising in light disgust. 'Sorry,' I said.

'It's fine,' she said. Her eyes were still clear, but mocked me, mimicking the earnest expression in my eyes. 'What do you do?' I asked her quickly changing the subject. 'I'm an architect,' she said. 'Independent or with a company?' I asked, noticing that her shoulders were at perfect distance from her stretched neck, her chin pointing at me, her arms folded under small breasts that pressed against the thin merino sweater. She stood with her legs slightly apart, her stockinged feet in flat but expensive sandals. The gold buckle on them was of a famous fashion house, possibly Parisian, but I couldn't place it and it irritated me like a scratch at the back of my throat.

Unusual, I thought, flats for a Delhi girl. I wondered if she had a back problem. But even more unusual was her choice of clothes. Every girl I could see was dressed in Indian wear, as if for their own wedding; the Diwali season affording them an opportunity to dress in lavishly embroidered saris or salwar kameez, heavy sets of diamonds, rubies, emeralds, embellishing ears, necks, hands and arms. 'Independent,' she said. Her eyes were laughing now, twinkling back the hundreds of diyas that burned solitarily in small earthen cups across the huge lawn. Some had burned out making tiny pools of comforting darkness amongst the incandescent gold hue. There were about fifteen or twenty card tables in the expansive L-shaped verandah of the house which was a mix of British colonial influence and jarring Mughal themes. At this time at night, nearly two o' clock, almost all of them were full with six to eight people at every table. The crystal bowls were full of hundred, five hundred, thousand rupee notes, and we could hear hoots of delight when someone won a big hand and shouts of despair when someone lost a seemingly winning round.

The clap and click of heavily adorned fingers called out for a refill of single malt or red wine, for samples of snacks, and a five hundred would be palmed for immediate and non-stop attention from the salivating waiters who were a little drunk themselves, their leering eyes shifting from the bowls of money to the low-cut blouses of the fabulously dressed women. I could see my friends. Most of the men and women sat at separate tables, the men playing bigger stakes, the women content with smaller numbers, instead flaunting their jewel encrusted necks above white chests and creamy skin.

'Your husband plays?' I said. 'Yes,' she pointed to his table. He was sitting with four men and two women. 'My friends, the girls and guys, always sit at different tables. It really annoys me. When I play, I like to play with the girls.' 'That didn't sound right at all,' she said laughing. 'Sorry? I didn't understand,' I said. And then immediately I said, 'Oh, come on, you're nitpicking.'

She smiled. 'Sorry, I've had a little too much to drink. So you're an architect, independent, young,' and motioning to her husband I continued, 'married. What kind of work do you do?' We were standing next to a gas heater and it was making me sweat on the back of my neck, and tiny drops of sweat darted down my spine. I wondered if it was making a mess of my white starched shirt. 'I design green buildings for free.'

'For free?'

'Yes. I am usually a consultant. I help architectural firms, as much as I possibly can.' She shrugged and carried on, 'It's mostly so that the clients can show off and be cool and with the programme, you know? But it's still a good thing.'

She shrugged again. 'So why not.' 'Yes. Very good thing. And all that. But for free? Why? How? How come?' She smiled. 'I learnt how to make buildings more efficient. Seventy percent of my clients would never pay an architectural firm to get an expert like me. So I do it for free. It helps get me work and it is good for the environment. I don't need the money. So why not.' 'Wow,' I said. 'Wow.' I repeated, a trifle distracted by the damp patch about my collar.

I moved slowly in a gentle arc neither wanting to break the flow of conversation, nor willing to show my apparently sodden back. She didn't react. Her clear eyes looked straight into mine. 'Do you want to go play?' I motioned towards the tables. 'No. I don't play. But by all means, please carry on. Nice meeting you.' And she turned towards the bar. 'No, no. I don't play. I mean I don't really play. I play sometimes, just a hand or two.' She interrupted, 'Yes, you play with the girls.' 'Yes. You're right. I do. And you're right, that doesn't sound right.' We both laughed. One more diya out of the four-hundred-and-thirty-seven extinguished itself.

'Drink?' I asked.

'Yes please,' she replied. 'Jack and Coke.'

'Diet coke?' I enquired knowingly.

'Coke please.'

'You are probably one of the few girls, perhaps one of the last people in Delhi who drink coke and not diet coke,' I said admiringly.

She didn't say anything, the corners of her mouth turned in a questioning smile. She was making me nervous.

I got myself a jack and coke as well, chucking the last bit of wine on the dewy grass. I leaned against the pleated pink satin folds of the bar and said, 'How do you know the hosts?'

'My husband and Gaurav went to college at BU.'

'And his wife?'

'I don't know his wife.'

'She's a bitch, his wife,' I said pointing towards a thin girl in a white Herve Leger dress, circulating the tables, air kissing the guests, her bleached hair reflected the flames of the diyas when she threw her head back in exaggerated laughter at every table. She always extended her left hand forward to say hello, flashing her 10-carat diamond which was the subject of many oohs and aahs at every party, and especially today in her own domain, in her 15-acre farmhouse, her conceit and arrogance whirled about her like the cigar smoke that hung thick and heavy above the tables.

'That's rude. You are a little drunk,' she was amused. Her eyes twinkled the evening colours of Diwali at me. I could hear fireworks in the distance from another party, perhaps a competing party, I mused.

Earlier in the evening I had lit some sparklers and firecrackers at my own farmhouse which was not too far from Gaurav's house. My mother insisted that we light a few, for *shagun*, even if I didn't want to celebrate Diwali the way I had, boisterously, for thirty years. The puja preceding that had been unusually silent and solemn, devoid of my father's usual jokes. The air wafted with the intoxicating smell of sandalwood incense, velvety with awareness that my wife was no longer present, her bright, cheerful face wasn't there, the face that always shone brighter than the gods.

My mother led the *aarti,* her voice of soft notes made my skin prickle as I looked about the small puja room, at the tightly-closed eyes of my father making worried wrinkles about his sorrowful face, at my sister and her husband who stood together, their arms interlaced and folded in prayer, at the dancing goddesses who looked through their slit eyes drunk with benevolence, the painted ceramic statues of Lakshmi and Ganesha who were centre stage today, the Guru Nanak and Sai Baba photographs relegated to the background where they could hardly be seen in the fog of the burning incense.

At the end of the *aarti* , in which I had not sung a single word, instead focussing on a spider that busied itself in the corner of the ceiling, my eyes burned with grief, my jaws clenched with the mistakes that had cost me the cosseting tenderness of my imperfect marriage.

All our eyes were wet, and it was easy to shift the awkward grief to the too many incense that had been lit by my mournful, troubled mother. I tried to make small jokes at the end, but the murmurs of polite sounds only made me realize how much my wife was missed by my family.

I wished then, looking at the gods around me, gods that did nothing but stare out of their gilded frames and carved thrones, that I was dead.

At least she would have been here if I were dead, I thought. A widow perhaps, but with a family that loved her, a family that would have helped her remarry in a respectful year, a family that today on Diwali was disappointed with me, their anger curdling beneath the resigned truth that I was, after all, their blood.

I touched my parent's feet and I wondered what she was doing at that very moment. Perhaps she was singing the *aarti* in her house, perhaps her parents looked on sadly too, perhaps they had forgotten about me as they sang determinedly in fiery unison.

As we trooped out of the puja room, a procession I remember my wife had led a year ago holding the *aarti thali*, I remembered the trinkets of her anklets making colourful sounds against the refurbished marble flooring. She was the only girl I had ever known to wear anklets with her Indian wear.

The crack of a rocket shook me out of my thoughts and the moonless sky above lit up in gold shimmering stars. Everyone at the tables clapped and hooted, impatience evident in the token claps of those who wanted to continue their hand, greedily eyeing the bowls of money before them.

One after another, rockets shot up in the sky, many at the same time, dyeing the blackened smog of Delhi in a rainbow of colours. The sky above heaved with smoke, dazzles and glitters.

'I wonder how many servants are doing this,' I said. 'Ten, perhaps more?' I continued looking quizzically at the sky at the dozen or so blooms of sparkling showers.

'Maybe,' she said.

'I want to go see. Will you come?'

'You want to go all the way to their back garden to see how many servants are doing this?' she said looking at me with curious surprise, soft laughter escaping her thin lips.

'Why not?' I said. 'They are lighting up our sky, aren't they?'

'It's their sky too, you know,' she said.

'Not in this city,' I said pointing at the card tables, 'In this city it's *their* sky.'

We walked around the house, some at the tables called out our names, raising glasses of champagne and whiskey. 'Wish me luck,' one shouted.

'Sit with me, you old bastard,' said another.

'Deepa, come join us!' came another shout.

'Deepa.' I said. 'Your name is Deepa.'

'Yes,' she said, this time looking at me with quiet compassion.

'Deepa,' I repeated. 'What a wonderful name. What a coincidence. Diwali. Diyas. Deepa.'

'Deepa,' I said again feeling the sound of her name, tasting the two simple syllables in my mouth.

'You're drunk,' she said pulling at the crook of my elbow. Her fingers felt kind.

'You don't want to know my name?'

'Aditya. Aditya,' she repeated.

'You know my name,' I said, flattered.

'Don't be flattered,' she said. 'The bartender took your name, Mr Aditya.'

When she said 'Mr Aditya' she said it with a touch of contempt.

'Oh,' I said, my voice dropping low, her fingers still guiding me by my elbow.

We walked quietly, the sound of the music, laughter and swish of cards being dealt grew distant and the crack of the rockets came closer and louder. The sound was startling each time, but also encouraging, pulling us closer, like a magnetic field of promises and secrets. The grass crunched under our feet and she removed her flats.

'Why?' I asked.

'They are getting wet. May as well carry them. Besides grass speaks to you when you walk barefoot.'

I raised my eyebrows in deliberate amazement, and then raised my glass to her, emptying it in my mouth and partially down my shirt.

'How come you're wearing flats? I mean it's unusual to see a Delhi girl in anything but towering stilettos.'

'Delhi isn't only the girls you've met, Aditya.'

I threw the glass in the inky distance and it landed with a soft thud. On grass, I thought gratefully.

'You know, you are no different from that crowd you seem to hate,' she said.

'I never said I hated them. Many of them are my best friends. And yes, I am no different.'

'But you want to be,' she said.

'So do you.'

I could make out a white tent where the caterer's kitchen had been set up and the sound of hissing oil and clanging utensils echoed in the hushed air. The harsh light from the tent spilled onto the grass, unkempt and rowdy here, far away from the combed, pruned grass in the front. Deepa's feet were nearly invisible in their grabbing blades.

Through the gaps in the pleated white folds of the tent, I could make out six men cooking and chopping, shouting instructions in Hindi with every sentence accessorised with creative cursing. I laughed appreciatively. Deepa raised her eyebrows and shook her head.

'What?' I said. 'Don't like the way the common man speaks?'

'You all speak like that,' she said waving back at the house. 'All men do. All Delhi men.' She stressed on 'Delhi' and let go of my elbow. I felt unsteady without her support, and my heart suddenly ached.

Some of them must have heard us or seen us, because they quietened down.

'We scared them,' I said.

'We always do,' she replied.

'So what happened? Why did you break up with your wife?'

'I didn't say I broke up,' I said, irritated at the hint of condescension in her voice and more so because she was right.

'I don't really want to talk about it.' I was beginning to slur.

She didn't say anything.

'There was no love. Okay? There was no love.'

'No love is no reason to break a heart.'

'That's what they all said,' I lied, surprised by her choice of words.

Twirling around, my arms raised, my palms upturned to a scarred, leukodermic sky, I repeated, 'That's what they all said.'

We could smell the pungent sharpness of the beedi smoke and the laughter of a dozen men fifteen feet ahead of us crowding around crackers that they lit raucously with candles, matches and beedis. Rockets whizzed past their foreheads in uncaring, reckless audaciousness. A few of them noticed us, but unlike the caterers they didn't lower their voices. They carried on their banter, their laughter almost menacing.

'Come,' she said. 'Let's go back.'

I nodded silently. I was aware that I wanted to kiss her immediately. It was an urgent sensation, and I could feel it in my knees. She knew it too. She licked her upper lip and although she didn't look at me, her face had a searching expression, her hands interlaced behind her neck, her elbows touched in front of her breasts.

We walked back silently, the back of our hands brushing against each other every few steps. I kept looking at her as though wanting to say something. She returned my look once or twice, lightly shaking her head, the corner of her mouth upturned in an easy smile.

The house seemed closer now on our way back. I stopped, turning towards her, reaching out for her forearm. We looked at each other, aware of the hungry tension between us. I pulled her to me, my thighs against her tweed skirt. I looked into those clear eyes that were empty of their mischievous humour, and leaned to kiss her. Just as I reached her lips, she turned her head. I found myself lost in the darkness of her perfumed hair. She placed her hands on my chest and pulled back.

'I… ' I began to speak.

'Don't say anything,' she said. She held my arm and slipped back into her flats.

We walked, this time with some deliberate distance, our hands no longer touching. I wanted to come closer, wishing I hadn't tried to kiss her. I looked at her, but she wouldn't look at me, her determined strides neither fast nor slow.

'How come I haven't seen you before?' I asked suddenly, aware that we were walking towards her husband's table.

It was three thirty now and some of the tables had emptied out, only the vestiges of half drunken whiskey glasses, toothpicks and jumbled cards scattered about on them.

'Perhaps Delhi is not that small,' she said raising her glass in acknowledgement towards me.

' Perhaps,' I said. 'Will I see you...'

But she silenced me with a smile that held me back.

We weaved through empty and half-full tables, the gold organza table cloths sullied with kebabs and wine.

'Hi,' she said placing her hand on her husband's broad shoulder.

'Hi baby,' he replied through the cigarette dangling from his lips, looking at his cards disdainfully.

'You haven't brought me luck,' he said.

'No, I haven't,' she replied, 'but I brought you Aditya.'

I stuck out my hand.

'Anurag,' he said removing his left hand from the cards and shaking my hand crookedly, barely looking up from his cards and contemplation.

'Join us,' he said.

'No, thank you.' I said.

'He only plays with girls,' Deepa said, her chin resting on his bald head.

'Plays with girls? Plays with girls!' he said and the entire table laughed.

'I think I'll get another drink,' I said, walking away past the four-hundred-and-thirty-seven diyas, all of which had burned themselves out.

At the Eye Doctor

My eyes closed and my head resting on my wife's shoulder, I could feel the supple and gentle softness of her shoulder. Her cashmere sweater tickled my beard and my cheek warmed against her.

We were in the eye doctor's waiting room. He had asked his secretary – not a qualified nurse practitioner – to dilate my eyes three times in a period of thirty minutes. Each time the secretary got up with a sigh, setting down the pencil that twirled in his hand as if it were performing a private circus of its own, pulled my eyelids roughly as he squeezed sharp drops in them. In that half hour, with my head rising and falling with the pleasant motion of my wife's breathing, I wished several times that this would last forever.

The room was tiny, at most 70 square feet, and if I so much as stretched my legs I would hit a pale wooden bench that lined the opposite wall, just like the one that I sat on. The bench had a surprisingly deep cushion, and I was grateful for the comfort it offered me, just as it must have offered to thousands who must have waited in this room, adorned disconcertingly with too many prayer thoughts and psalms for a doctor and much too many certificates in his praise.

I would not think that an eye doctor's expertise was any less than that of a cancer specialist or a heart surgeon, but this room elevated him to an unnecessarily exalted position, as if he were saving lives every day, veneering over the actual hackneyed disposition of an eye doctor. He was an excellent doctor no doubt, but a doctor who was disappointed that his talents came to little better use than to write out prescriptions for yet another set of spectacles. When he did find something major, like glaucoma or night blindness, that day he would pause in his waiting room, paying homage to the certificates, sighing with gratefulness to Lakshmi, Shiva, Hanuman and Ganesha. His secretary looked at him with reverence then, as the doctor looked with reverence at the frescoed gods, and this way the waiting room was a temple for both men.

I pulled my baseball cap lower over my forehead, spots and colours making squiggles and puzzles inside my eyelids. I tried to shut them from my mind, instead happy to concentrate on the millions of tickling fibres making love with my beard, my sharp cheekbone digging inside her shoulder. We whispered small jokes to each other. I laughed, pulling my cap even lower, feeling the eyes of others in this cubicle of a room, but also proud, imagining envious stares towards us, a couple, truly in rare love, my beautiful wife and the handsome me. Together, we held more pull and draw in this waiting room than the tinted ceramic and metal gods, the painted mantras in italic letters and garish colours, the bold certificates from known and unknown universities in gilded frames.

She whispered small stories to me in sentences filled with everyday conversation about clothes, music and work, her voice was comforting and her breath was sweet and warm. I thought about the previous night when we dined at the most stylish restaurant in Delhi with its canopies shaped like birds of paradise, the gold-leafed ceilings that made intimate domes around small spaces where we sat together, our thighs touching in the velvet loveseat, our elbows occasionally brushing while we had lobster bisque and rocket salad. The pianist, a man who looked much too old and a little too sad for forty-five, came to us many times for requests, a habit I found vaguely flattering, embarrassing and occasionally annoying. He was familiar with us since we ate there often and always clapped after each song and too loudly after a bottle of wine. We always sent him several glasses of champagne in appreciation. Last night too, he came many times, his face bathed in the warm glow of gold from the ceiling, crinkling in a broad white-toothed smile that made deep rivers of skin, blackened tributaries where the gold light never reached. He played all our favourites, hackneyed classics that everyone had heard, the ticket to sage nodding about interest and knowledge in classical music. The Blue Danube, SwanLake, Fur Elise, Nut Cracker floated in the room, their end notes receiving scattered applause, an applause that was always led by and ended with the sound of my wife's clapping, distinct in the brushing sound they made as the fingers interlaced with every clap, the palms cupped lightly against each other.

We were served food in Cristofle crockery and we swirled the wine, an expensive and heavy Bordeaux, from the skyscraper stems of Schmidt glasses, and I looked at my wife, distracted as she always was when the waiters busied around our table setting down foie gras for me and caviar for her. She looked perfect last night, she was mine and I had never been more in love. With every blink of her deep brown eyes I thanked the gods that she was mine forever, marvelling at the perfection of our relationship, at the completeness we offered each other, at the effortless oneness of our being. When the waiters had finally departed with much bowing, and expressive smiles, more towards her than me, I looked at her and said, 'I love you.' And I repeated it again and again till she closed her lips around mine, emptying the wine that was in her mouth, and a streak of red escaped my mouth and made a tiny blot of crimson on my starched white collar. We made small talk sound sensitive and we made their banality disappear as we clinked glasses and listened to each other carefully. Much before the end of dessert, by which time we had finished two bottles, I could not wait to go home and make love to this woman, this wife of mine of one year, this wife that I could hardly believe was besotted by me. The syrupy rivulets of the chocolate dessert made its way down slowly to my stomach as the car zoomed through the nearly bare roads of Delhi at 2 a.m., and the ragpickers laughed with their heavy loads scattered about them, the streetlights were high and hazy, and empty buses made their way to not-so-empty depots as despondent conductors spat dredges of tobacco from red lips that chewed in contemplation, ruminating in peace.

My driver had caught my eye awkwardly in the rear-view mirror between kisses that we stole in the backseat, but I was uncaring and unembarrassed because of the heavy Bordeaux, and continued to kiss as we passed cars that sagged under the weight of weary families and mismatched suitcases that entered Delhi for the first time from far away villages.

In our kisses I dreamt of having a baby with her soon, and she would bear us both a son, of that I was sure, a son I would name Armaan, a son who would be followed two years later by a daughter.

Yes, that would be perfect, I thought.

We would be the perfect urban Indian family. The perfect example of a progressing, prospering India. I continued to dream as her mouth became wetter and her knees tightened against mine. One day as a family we would come to Odyssey, the restaurant where we had dined, and one day my son would throw us a surprise party there for our twenty-fifth anniversary. It was going to be the perfect life. I was sure of it.

I passed a thousand rupee note as a tip to my driver for the late night work, and then on second thoughts, I gave him another thousand, bribing him to cast away his embarrassed yet aroused thoughts about us, and as men we exchanged that knowing glance. His held the promise that with the turn of his bike's ignition he would, with respectful servitude, leave behind those aroused thoughts at my threshold, and that he as a driver could not and would not dream of my wife when he made love to his own.

That was the look in his eyes, in his silent promise, and I had decidedly paid him well for that.

When we made love that night I could taste the Davidoff on her skin, men's Davidoff, the only fragrance that she wore, and the smell of Davidoff mixed with the perspiration of our skin, the stained wine on our tongues and the chocolate dessert in the cracks of our lips. We fell asleep entwined, our smiling faces turned towards each other, and my last look before I fell asleep contentedly was towards the thumb-sized gold Ganesha on her bedside who smiled benevolently at us, for only with his blessings had it been possible for us to be together.

The next day at work, she had reminded me of the eye doctor's appointment with a gentle and loving text message and in turn I asked her to come with me. The doctor suspected I needed glasses, but to be sure dilation was necessary. He asked me if I had forty-five minutes to spare and I did not, but at my wife's sweet insistence, I cancelled the last few meetings of the day, happy to please her, and even happier to rest my head on her twenty-eight year old shoulder, the age difference between us a little perturbing for her family, a difference that was easily bridged by my station in life. While she came from a wealthy business family herself, I was wealthier, a fact I could see in the impressed satisfaction in her father's eyes. Her father was barely fifty-two, fourteen years older than me, yet I called him Papa, and I touched his feet when he gave his blessings. Her mother was where my wife's radiant looks came from and I felt appreciative towards her.

Patients came and went, and I could tell most of them were happy as they left, the lightness in their step evident, making their way out in the sliver of space between the wooden benches. I shifted uncomfortably as the cushion no longer felt as soft as it had in the beginning. To pass time I asked her to tell me silly stories about her school life and so she lent me slightly boring details that did not interest me much, although the velvety sound of her voice floated in my head like the swirls of the incense stick that burned in the corner of this little room.

She talked and I was nearly lost in a dream that lay halfway between awake and asleep when I sensed a tightening in her voice and a quiver in her shoulder. I didn't think anything of it except that her sentences immediately became shorter and her story seemed to lose intimacy and excitement, banal as it may already have been. My eyes closed, I listened to the sudden mechanical voice that eventually died into silence.

I raised my head in concern and although I could not open my eyes, I looked towards her questioningly, a gesture that was met with her patting my head back on her shoulder, a touch too protective as her fingers rested about my eyes.

'What happened?' I said.

'Nothing,' she replied, the two syllables spoken with unnecessary lilt and inflection.

I knew she was lying to me. Had her thoughts about school and adolescence touched a raw nerve? Was it something that I might have inadvertently said in my dreaming plait of thoughts? Had she sensed that I was not quite listening to her? What could it be? Confessing, I apologized for my inattentiveness and no sooner had three sentences escaped my mouth, her fingers from my eyes dropped to my lips, as if silencing me.

Minutes of uncomfortable silence later, she spoke in my ear and said that her ex-fiancée, a man whom she was briefly engaged to, had entered the room at the time.

He was now in the doctor's room, she said.

I stiffened but kept what I thought was mature composure. But she felt the immediate difference, just as I had, and she cooed soft unnecessary words of endearments in my ear, words that normally cocooned me in their warmth and love, words that instead sounded patronising and irritating now. She whispered the usual comforts that any wife would in this situation, and it compounded my irritation. I said it was 'nothing', but the word sounded as unconvincing to my ears as her 'nothing' had.

Together we resigned ourselves to the odd, uncomfortable silence between us, only the irksome clicking of my heel against the wooden flooring audible, the waiting room empty this late in the evening, even the heavy breathing of the secretary drifting into sleep with the close of the day.

The thoughts of Odyssey seemed distant, the thoughts of our lovemaking uninteresting and dry. The cashmere no longer tickled me with sensuous delight, and her fingertips on my cheek felt heavy and laden. I lifted my head from her shoulders and crossed my arms in my lap. I imagined her look of pleading dismay, her mouth opening to say something, and then closing in hopelessness.

He had ripped open the sheathing that I had so lovingly created and sewn tightly over her wounds, wounds that were of a past that no longer belonged to her because they did not belong to us.

My wife, Madhuri Gupta, was Maduri Baniyal before she had married me. That she would change her last name was obvious, but at my mother's insistence the 'h' had been added to her first name as well. The priest who had been consulted before our wedding had in fact asked for a complete change of name, to begin her name with a K, a fact that was agreed by a distant Uncle who was a famed numerologist, but I had pleaded with the priest to make the change more convenient, a possibility that was made easier with the packet of five thousand that I had firmly deposited in his saffron kurta. He gave my mother the option of adding the H. This made us align quite perfectly, he said, and my mother had agreed with a stiff lip and an upturned face.

At the wedding the priest had winked at my wife and said that she should be grateful for such a practical husband, a sentence that was met with my wife's ready acquiescence and laughter. I was filled with gratitude that she was not like the wives of my friends, all of them a touch too clever, and in fact rebellious.

I had proudly looked at my bride, the perfect modern Indian woman. A photograph of ours at the wedding captured that moment. I am looking at her with proud adoration, smiling down at her as she smiled at the camera, but not directly, her eyes just averted from the viewer's gaze, eyes that were reserved to only look at me forever.

Madhuri as Maduri was involved with her ex-fiancée for five years before he had broken off their engagement. The reasons were unclear to me and apparently unclear to Madhuri as well. It was two months after her break-up that we were cheerfully introduced by my cousin at a party where Madhuri was more than a little tipsy, dancing alone amongst fairy lights and enormous Greek statues. We quickly grew close to each other. I was aware that she was still recovering from the trauma of a bad break-up. I fell in love with her, embittered towards this man, Prithvi, who had broken my Madhuri's heart, resentful that it had belonged to him for five years before he had trashed it in a bin. Over coffee, wine and long walks, I listened to her. Her words never sounded like tirades or outbursts, instead they were a symphony of a broken heart that could no longer sing.

I prayed every day like I had never prayed before for Madhuri to love me, and the sweep of her perfect skin would appear in my eyes as I prayed deeply. I gave up smoking as an offering to the gods. When she confessed to me that she was seeing a psychiatrist, I only prayed deeper. My prayers were finally heard and answered after a trip to Tirupathi, when at a dinner at Odyssey I mustered the courage to kiss her, clumsily, and she closed her eyes and kissed me back.

I thought of that first kiss now, not long ago – barely two years had passed.

The waiting room was suffocating me. The muffler around my neck felt like a noose and I loosened it, allowing some sweat to escape from my skin.

My eyes still closed, I could only hear the seconds that ticked away slowly on the Omega clock that hung above the secretary's head and the wistful, pained breathing of my wife. The door of the doctor's cabin opened and I raised my head in challenge. I sensed a pause in his step, as he surely must have looked from Madhuri to me, and the click of his shoes laughed at me and sneered at her.

When I opened my eyes the sky-blue walls of the room seemed white and the gods and certificates blurred as though untidily erased away. I looked at Madhuri, her skin was not as shiny as it was half an hour ago and her brown eyes were a little too desperate and fearful. I felt a pang of pity. To throw her a coin of comfort, I patted her head, and announced to the secretary that I would after all keep my business meetings, and I would return to the good doctor another day. I leaned on the word 'good' as I said it.

But, he insisted, the doctor was ready for me now and my eyes were dilated enough.

Another day, I said more authoritatively than him and I walked out, my vision hazy as I made my way down polished terrazzo steps that spiralled down.

In Bombay

I have always wanted to join the army. It seemed that it would make a man out of me. Not that I'm not a man, in fact I am, and I am more a man than most men I know. But it is also evident that men as soldiers are tough, conditioned to pain and death, weather and war. In pain a man truly becomes a man. As in love.

Three years ago when it was a bitter weekend in Delhi and the weather was heavenly in Bombay, I was a mediocre architect living a mediocre life in Delhi. I am the same now. The monotony of my daily life had weathered my exterior to crumbling paper and my insides were molten with the stale, desolate air of Delhi. For me, Delhi held no promises ... the city was beaten and tired. Just as I was.

In an extraordinary act of kindness my best friend Samir, who lived a perpetually fanciful life under rainbow clouds gilded with gold, invited me to a party in Bombay that he was attending with his wife, Naintara and her sister Apsara. As usual I had declined his invitation, but Samir had persisted through the week. A man not easy to say no to, he insisted that he drag me away from my shell of banality to what he promised would at least be an interesting weekend.

Samir was the first and only real friend I ever had. We first met at the architectural school in Gurgaon we attended. He belonged to a family of architects and it was obvious to him, his parents, and his elder sister who had already joined the firm, that he would be one too.

For me, the choice to become an architect happened in eighth grade. That was the first time I had held a protractor in my hand and I knew I wanted to do something in which I would use this oddly beautiful instrument. It reminded me of me. It was incomplete, just like me. But it could also be useful. And so could I, I thought to myself, turning it this way and that, bending it till bright cracks formed in the cheap acrylic.

Samir and I appreciated each other's mediocre work. Me cautiously, in hesitant, awkwardly formed sentences since I never really knew how to give a compliment, and he with his usual vociferous enthusiasm. We weren't talented. It was our fate to be architects for reasons that were clear as the reflection in the mirror. When we graduated he asked me to join his firm, and although my first reaction was that of surprise, I also knew it was always meant to be this way.

That our mediocrity was accepted easily by him and uneasily by me made us better than awful and comfortably confident. We knew we would never design a world-class building, so we began to develop a sizeable business in what we were good at – designing high rise apartments and malls for mediocre albeit disgustingly wealthy real estate developers.

We travelled to Dubai and Milan for ideas. We asked our clients to pay for us and preferred it if they did not travel with us. We would design buildings that would have a hint of the freedom of the West, but encumbered and constrained to maximise space and minimise cost, our buildings like most new constructions in India looked shabbily second rate. But all this was masked over at grand launches attended by powerful politicians and Bollywood stars.

Other than our happily pedestrian professional lives that elicited praise from clients and family alike, including generous cash handouts that Samir's father pushed towards me in crisp white envelopes, our personal lives could not be more different. After work, usually after eight, I made my way to my two-bedroom rented apartment in Geetanjali Enclave, a tuck of rooms overlooking the Lado Sarai golf course. I would sit on the terrace, as I do now, smoking two cigarettes, sometimes reading, sometimes just looking at the sky, waiting for the serene moon to yawn its way high above and then I would retire to bed. Samir would make evening plans with Naintara and equally fancy friends for drinks at bars high above the city or in cosy, expensive restaurants where wine was served by gloved hands and where food was decorated like art.

Every weekend, Samir would ask me to join him and his rainbow friends in a tone that was both humorous and sincere. Every time my answer was a shake of my head and an exchange of smiles that made us both pause. He would shake my hand goodbye and hold it for an unnecessary second, smiling his lovely smile, and in those moments, I could sometimes glimpse what love might be.

You see, when I was born, premature, hairless, and extremely tiny, the gynaecologist with a stern affront and a much too hairy lip for a woman did tell my mother – a simple lady made of pink petals – that her son, her only child would be incapable of love. Apparently, in the half baked formation of my existence in my mother's precious womb of silk and skin, love had missed me in entirety. It hurt my mother deeply, as it would hurt any mother, but I think it hurt her more than usual, in that she cried for a full three-hundred-and-four days, at the end of which she died peacefully. The number of days as you would have correctly observed, is the number of chemicals needed to produce love. I hadn't any of them.

So, I have never loved. I feel what might be termed as mild affection for people who are deemed closest to me. As I have never loved, I have never been loved either. Although I do not know what love is, I understand and observe the signs of love, and empty of love as I might be, I am blessed with reasonable intelligence and what some, including my Samir, have called an acute sense of observation. I couldn't stand the hypocrisy and the pretensions of the love of aunts and uncles on birthdays that whisked by fast in an insipid childhood and the dreadfully boring letters and glitter-laden cards with heart shaped popouts presented in high school by shapeless girlfriends to satisfy their own femininity.

On the flight I was seated with Apsara. Across the aisle from us, Naintara cooed in Samir's ear, feeding him this and that, with words that sounded like distant bells, tiny bells that made me think of a European summer. I was fidgeting uncomfortably in the business class seat, unbuckling and buckling my seat belt right until take off, when Apsara put a surprisingly gentle hand on my oscillating knees and held me in a gaze that was both soft and direct, and when she looked away, we were already high above the streaming blooms of restive clouds.

Apsara's oval face changed colours as the sun rose on the distant horizon. The sun was a gentle peep of red at first, then a bright white disc of spotless light that made Apsara's pupils contract into pinpoints of deep black encircled by golden speckles of flickering browns. I had never seen the sun rise before and apparently neither had she, she exclaimed, her face pressed against the window. The loose brown strands that escaped from her carelessly tied curls burned golden against the window, and when she pulled away her eyes were moist with the harshness of the light, and a few crumbs of mascara dotted the swell of her pink cheeks. I wanted to reach out my hand to wipe away at her eyes, and she must have read my mind, because her eyes widened in surprise. But the mascara looked to belong there, in the nearly imperceptible crevasses of lines beneath her eyes. Crevasses that I wished I could be lost in, crevasses that would fold my life in security.

Apsara knew my genetic defect as she had been told by Samir. I preferred it if people knew, otherwise it was readily assumed that I was simply distant, cold and uninterested. In fact I was none of this, but since emotions ride with love, my incapability to show emotions made me seem like granite. But quickly Apsara made me forget about that. She made me forget about me. Neither did she converse in haltingly silly sentences nor was the conversation marked with a profusion of jokes that was always the case with ordinary people, as if testing me on humour and wondering what else I was incapable of.

Her words and questions flowed freely and I replied as best I could, hesitatingly, but even as I stammered and stuttered through the best conversation I ever had in my life, her look was open and steady, not the characteristic encouraging condescension that I received from everyone else.

Her sentences were long and full of concerned ifs and buts. Her laughter rang with easy appreciation and filled my ears with delicate warmth. She patted my arm lightly when the pace of words changed and tapped on my hand to make her point. Her eyelashes touched the corners of her eyelids when she was surprised. And she was surprised often. her eyes made soft creases about their corners that blossomed towards her veined ivory temples when she smiled. And she smiled often.

Upon landing I was sorry that our conversations with their many tributaries and unfulfilled endings had to come to an end. I realized that it was the first time I regretted the end of a conversation.

When she got up from her seat, a patch of her perspiration from her neck stained the red leather of the seat. Quietly, I swept it in my fingers, tasting it against my tongue.

Naintara and Apsara were the hosts of the party and they had to immediately busy themselves with the arrangements of the evening. I took to a corner of the hotel, drinking expensive champagne on Samir's tab and smoking cigarettes, making blue wisps of smoke that reminded me of the curls of Apsara's hair.

I thought about her words that reminded me, strangely, of running four-hundred metre races in school, races that made my heart pound, a heart that otherwise rested in comatose boredom.

I wondered at the new emotions that pushed against my chest and pulsated in my hands, and at the taste of her bitter sweat that glossed above the sweet champagne. I wondered if I was getting cured. And I immediately pushed these thoughts away from my mind, knowing it was impossible. Amputees do not grow limbs and I could not love.

The evening flowed with more champagne and fine wine. The guests encircled Naintara and Apsara, delighted at the party, astonished at their obvious beauty and charmed by their friendly words of praise and inquisitiveness. Samir stayed by Naintara's side, basking in her afterglow, radiant in her reflected glory. Even as I strayed in the corners of the party, away from the effusing crowd, Apsara pulled me in, into the whirlpool of people and their laughter. I was introduced to many people, people who did not know me and my unusual disease. They asked about my work and business and I replied with halting confidence.

Distant as I cannot help but be, that night in Bombay, I smiled as I was led by her hand that was made of three-hundred-and-four roses, the softness of which made the hair on my wrist bristle and my fingers tremble. She looked at me and she smiled back. In her smile the party paused, the conversations stopped, the waiters in their penguin tails froze, and everything that I knew about myself shot from underneath me.

I have always been much too aware of time and its resonate steady ticks. The evening passed as all else does, and I found myself sitting at the corner of the pool with Apsara, her ankles of impossible beauty skimming the water. Every time her feet touched the water, the water shimmered and shivered with pleasure. The moon, not quite full, glowed generously, wishing upon itself that it was full that night.

I felt like the moon that night. I wished that I wasn't the protractor I prized. I wished I could be the man she would want. I wished I could be the man I wanted to be. Now, three years later when I see a waxing, gibbous moon, I think of her, that night and what it would be like to be full and in her arms.

Karan and Maneck

As Karan and his father sat, not at ease, but sat rather pompously, heavily, in the S-Class Mercedes, it started raining. The heavy doors slapped aggressively and the driver rushed around the car, quickly wearing his peaked cap – a military mockery – the red braids a little dirty, Karan noticed as the car drove out of the Nigam Bodh Ghat cremation ground.

Just as well that they had left when they did, Karan thought, watching the rain pelting down in heavy droves, slashing across the car. His father lit a cigarette, clicking away impatiently on his cell phone, calling his stock broker, his voice lost in the corners of the car. Karan looked out of the rain-streaked, tinted windows, the hurrying, wet Delhi scurrying for cover, taking shelter under flyovers and bridges, the cars splashing reddened water, the water of wastes and people, water that Delhi fought over.

Their chief marketing officer's mother had died and the formality had to be kept, like dried flowers in a forgotten vase that occupies the powder rooms of five star hotels, and graces the dining tables of middle-class homes; that formality of a visit to the cremation ground had to be kept. The perfunctory bowed head, the bored mind, the quick 'Namaste' to the sweltering people under the humid sky, men drenched in sweat, their sweat making puddle marks around their vests, women wiping their sweat and tears with the palloo of their saris. Their colleagues – employees really, the word colleague was a pretense of hypocritical diplomacy – encircled Karan and his father, shaking hands, smiling shyly, acknowledging the richer men's presence, the relatives whispering in each other's ears and pointing, some menacingly, others with open admiration and envy, even as the cool wind fanned them and the burning bodies all around, soft ash settling on them like powdery snow, leaving silvery traces on Karan's shirt as he brushed away other people's death.

Looking out of the window he felt an immense sadness that enveloped him like the grey clouds above, and Karan started to think about the empty satisfaction of being rich, his dreams shattered, drowned and disappeared with the death of his friend Maneck.

Anyone who knew Karan, even faintly, knew he loved to talk about Maneck. Talk is a better word than brag, a different word, a different meaning, but it was almost bragging at first, like the torrential waves of a Turner landscape that strikes the eye from the foreground of the canvas, but there is much to that landscape, the glowing corner of the canvas, the distant people, the conversations you can almost hear if you press your ear to the painting. But just then, the museum guards stop the magic, your magic, as they tell you to take a step back, a step away from the velvet rope; for Karan a step away from Maneck.

Karan thought of Maneck as the rain kicked a thousand knocks on the car and the thunderous skies clapped with lightning. He listened to Maneck's laughing voice in his mind, his face intermingling with the inside elbow of the girl he loved the most in the world: Karan's only child, his daughter, Naina, her bare arms of coffee and butter, the small mole in the inside elbow, at that very undefined point where the arm twists to make the more firm outline of a forearm. When Karan was with her he couldn't look away, Naina cheerfully blissful in a world that Karan was afraid would tip him over. Sometimes he wished that it would.

Maneck and Karan were introduced twelve years ago in the fall. Delhi hardly has a fall, it is more an occasion for the acrid heat to turn gloomy, and the initial hint of winter is first felt on cool marble floors rather than the wind. It was September.

Karan remembered the smell in Maneck's room when they were waiting for his body to be brought home. One last time. Dead. The smell in the room was not the familiar smell of books and whiskey. It smelled of soap. The floor had been freshly washed because the bed had been pushed to the side against the wall, making way for the body. Maneck's body. A dead body is unfit to be placed on a bed. It must be put on the floor, against the hard cemented floor, and perhaps even more so because Maneck was an accident victim – a man who is a victim of an accident, a victim because the man is dead, a true victim, more specifically a car accident victim, and the body of a car accident victim must be placed on the floor because floors are easier to clean just in case any blood or fluids poured from his orifices, and if he were placed on a mattress then throwing out a bloody mattress would be macabre and add unnecessarily to the already tragic and horrifyingly sad morning.

Some stood, some sat, Karan leaned against the wall watching Maneck's boyfriend splayed against the soaped floor like an X, hugging the floor, clawing at it desperately as if it would, or should engulf him and take him to Maneck.

There were voices from the stairwell, and they were saying 'slowly, slowly', as the gurney turned uncomfortably through the narrow staircase and landings. Bodies – living bodies, pushing, yanking, grunting under Maneck's light weight, it was awkward on that staircase, but they continued carefully, carrying his already damaged body.

Maneck – battered, bruised, torn, soft and dead. Soft when Karan hugged him, because the ribs were broken and had punctured his lungs when the truck smashed into the car with five people inside, people who were seconds later a mangled, broken, shattered heap of bodies.

His father broke his thoughts.

'ITC would be a good share to buy now. Karan, are you listening?'

'Sorry Dad. Yes, ITC is always good. That's what you always say.'

'This cigarette is manufactured by ITC. The hotel where we entertain is owned by ITC.'

ITC is killing you, thought Karan. It is a good share to buy though. It makes money for you while you are alive.

They were crossing the WHO building, its blue projections fading, the many flags flapping in panic against the maniacal wind. Imagine a world without countries, Karan thought, and just as he did, the flags did tear up, slowly, one by one, rising high against the blackening sky, flying higher and higher, looking like free kites, dancing and twisting around each other, till they all became a medley of colours, and like fresh watercolour, they disappeared against the pregnant, howling clouds. He looked at the empty poles, erect, naked, bereft of their pride, and began to point excitedly but his father shushed him with a dismissing wave, already in conversation with the stock broker. The air inside the car was heavy with stale smoke, lingering at the windows, making blue patterns of snow molecules. Karan couldn't open the window, it was raining too hard. A crack would be a breach. A breach of calf leather and crore-rupee deals. Karan craned his neck to see the last of the WHO building, the flag poles aligning behind each other as the car swung, one pole behind the other, till he could only see only one pole, white and empty.

They always had Bloody Mary at The Buck Stops Here. Sometimes Maneck would have a whiskey, drinking deeply, smoking quietly, as he listened to Karan chatter. They would point around the restaurant at the colourful walls adorned with quotable quotes, and Karan would listen to Maneck talk about Voltaire, Napoleon and Descartes. He would speak in a voice that reminded Karan of chimes and school bells, his sentences informative and brief, his fingers spread across the Bloody-Mary-stained table cloth, gently reaching out for the tips of Karan's fingers as he looked at him with colourful eyes reflecting the quotes on the walls, his mouth playfully young and his ready smile swallowing every word that Karan said. Maneck would call him *jaan*.

That word would ring in Karan's mind when he first looked at Naina, he thought of that word, jaan, and thought of Maneck's face at The Buck Stops Here, his lingering fingers, his widening smile, his eyes of anticipation as the drinks were set down on stained table cloths. He named her Naina for her eyes, and he imagined that they would shine with the same sparkle as Maneck, eyes that taught him everything, eyes that loved him everywhere.

Karan remembered looking at Maneck's cut face, his skin wet and cold, his mouth ajar, that lovely mouth of promises and kisses, of truths and loves, of coiled emotions and pursed delight, of knowledge and spreading laughter. Now, that mouth of Maneck's was ajar in shock, in dismay, in realization that he would be dead in a second, in a life that was far from complete, in a life that he had only just begun, a life that he loved so much. Karan bent over him catching Maneck's face in snatching snapshots of visions, as many friends and family touched him and kissed him, stroking his drenched hair, caressing his forehead. Karan could guess why he was so wet. He had been clammed shut in a refrigerator, a horizontal refrigerator. The fleeting thought sickened his tearing, desperate mind. Those colourful eyes had been donated, the lids barely closed over the dismissively stuffed cotton wool.

The Mercedes banked like a plane on the wet road passing Sunder Nagar, the neat row of old houses shuddering under the weight of a weary sky. His thoughts alternated between Naina's eyes and Maneck's. They would have loved each other, he thought, and now Naina would never know him, and Maneck would never know my precious jaan, Naina.

His father interrupted his thoughts by demanding to know of the housing schedule for the factory workers at their cement plant. Karan answered distantly but obediently. A thirty-nine-year-old child, a child with a plant to play with and houses to make for workers no one cared about. It was only a pretence of magnanimity, of clinking glasses and of boastful conversations. Profit. Cash flow. Money. Karan felt that familiar sense of disgust entwine his punctured heart, threatening to puncture it further, deeper and forever.

The rain started to exhaust itself out. The relentless clatter reduced to a splashing symphony, playing notes that seemed clearer now, dipping with the memories of Maneck laughing against colourful walls. His throat would rise in laughter, and the chain of tiny metal balls that he wore would clink together as he talked animatedly of passion and the passion of passion itself. Karan remembered Maneck urging him to have that passion in their exactly sixty-three conversations. He screamed at him to have sex with a million people, he despaired at his banal ambitions and rotting, bourgeoise claims of travel and safari. He asked him to read everything, he smiled at him when they listened to anything. He urged him to run away and run far, to climb the highest mountains, to sleep on busy roads in a foreign land. He wanted to do all this together; he wanted to do everything now. He talked of exploring the world, of marching past hostile borders, of reporting the horrors of forgotten wars. He wanted to film, write, learn, and record everything. He would talk about cells and biology and make squiggly figures on paper napkins explaining to an awestruck Karan the insides of an atom. He would talk of evolution and of migrating birds. He would talk of the Enlightenment, and of India's independence. His lips moved fast with an automatic memory, a fascinating open and close of pink lips making the most delicious words and sentences about enchanting worlds. Worlds that Karan wanted to be a part of. Worlds that Maneck hugged him close to. Worlds that were dreams now.

Karan remembered the boat. A quiver ran up his arms. He remembered thinking about the women he had loved and the girls he had slept with before they became women and he a man, as he had looked down at the big hessian sack rocking gently. A sack for flour and grain. Now, a sack full of Maneck's ashes and bits of bone. The thoughts crossed Karan's barren mind.

Earlier that same day, at dawn, the hot young light of April had started to spread through the winding road through which they were driving, the light moving just ahead of the car, the light spreading evenly across Delhi just as the car reached the cremation ground. Five of Maneck's friends limped out, sodden with grief, their eyes heavy with twisted sleep. Karan walked ahead and alone, through gates where old priests sat smoking and coughing, guarding the burning bodies and the black smouldering ashes. There was no Maneck, not even battered and torn, just an even heap of ash and bones where they had left him burning through the stacked kindled wood, burning alone. Karan had watched the coiling flames painting glorious landscapes of colour as Maneck burned with passion for the last time. It had barely been eighteen hours since they had brought him here, and exactly twenty-four since he had been woken up with the call that Maneck was dead.

The smell was of boiled bones and marrow, a smell Karan was familiar with, but at the cremation ground it rose pungently like thick chicken soup, boiling and brewing. The smell of comfort food and home cooking streaked across his forehead like a racing memory as he looked down at the black, white, grey dust that still steamed. The last wisps of passion rose up to Karan as he held back craving tears, biting his lip, wiping them on his collar, not wanting his tears to sizzle on the hot ash as he picked out the bigger pieces of bones to be separated into a smaller red bag. The tips of his fingers burned as he sorted through the ash. Karan picked out a vertebra and looked at it closely, imagining his own vertebra attached to his full skeleton, protected from smashing trucks and cremation grounds, and suddenly he desperately wanted to kiss it, kiss Maneck, hold him, keep him. He continued to look at the dusty white bone for a few silent seconds and then placed it gently, his burning fingers lingering against it inside the small red bag.

His father was quiet and asleep. The driver's shoulders seemed to relax as he matched Karan's eyes in the rear-view mirror. He grinned slightly as if sharing a private joke. Bereft of his father's authoritative drone, the hum of the car made a peaceful duet with the clicking rain.

The day they packed Maneck into two sacks, one big hessian, and the smaller red bag, it had rained gently too. Karan remembered counting drops on the window, on the way to the river, and he began to count drops now. Through the drops, Karan could see an inverted Delhi passing by, traces of crumbling monuments near Nizamuddin and broken slums flooded with sewage flashed by. An inverted city inverted by drops from the forgiving sky. The drops traced out Naina's name, her eight-year-old face full of laughter and promises, her pink cheeks bubbling with her vivacious smile as she asked precocious questions about life and love. Thinking about her he wanted to jump out of the car, and run across the rain washed city into her always open arms. Instead he traced out her name and then Maneck's, thinking about her and him, thinking of Naina's birth, a year after Maneck was killed in the car crash.

As he traced her name and counted drops, he began to calculate how many hours till he would see her again. It was Wednesday and his visitations were on weekends and Tuesday evenings.

He had had a pizza dinner with her last night, and they had played dominoes splaying out in multicoloured tiles. At the end of the evening they were hugging and laughing on the floor, the dominoes scattered till the corners of the room like a starburst around them, pizza crumbs everywhere and at the corner of her lips, lips which he wiped gently with his spotless handkerchief, the corners of which had an 'N' embroidered in four colours. He had traced the fine hair at the tips of her eyebrows with his thumbs as he looked into her eyes of love and laughter and then kissed her forehead when it was time for her to go. The door shut behind her, leaving him to his emptiness and his hollow apartment that he had desperately fought for to gain independence from his parents. But the apartment seemed desultory and empty without her, so instead he smoothed his shirt and wore his cufflinks and walked to his car under the charcoaled clouds. As always, he went to his favourite bar at the Taj and got drunk, drunk enough to bear to go back home, his heart dappled with longing, his mind riding the confusing euphoria of alcohol.

His father was snoring gently, his phone unusually silent. They were passing the Lodi cremation ground in south Delhi, well situated for the upper-middle class and richer neighbourhoods. The parking lot of the cremation ground was packed, and the cars spilled out onto the streets, causing a traffic holdup. They slowed to a crawl and the blaring of the horns drowned the grief of the aggrieved. Looking at the chaos around him, Karan thought it was nice that Maneck was cremated in a small cremation ground near the river, a scattering of trees, goats and cows around the small plot. It was mostly quiet then and the city was distant as they packed him and sailed with him, ashes and bones, in a dinghy, in the filthy but tranquil Yamuna.

Karan looked over at his father. He looked restless even in his sleep, Karan thought. Looking at him, he tried to imagine him as a young man and a new father. The photographs he had seen of a younger, slimmer father never quite seemed to fit. .

At The Buck Stops Here the words were always easy with Maneck. In the incoherence of many thoughts and the multi-layered conversations, they would talk as the tables around them turned over many times. Karan would look at the glittering Maneck, Karan and Maneck, not just friends and unfortunately not lovers, a relationship preciously and perpetually on the bridge between desperate wanting and unabashed giving.

No one ever loved the way they did. After Maneck died, he was left to love alone with the love he had to give and the unending love that Maneck had given him, love that he wanted to empty out and expand. But no one loved him the way Maneck did and he tried desperately and urgently, trying to piece whatever he got from friends and lovers, emptying from his begging heart, the pieces of love like a jigsaw puzzle.

He looked down at his watch. Forty minutes had gone by since they had left Nigam Bodh Ghat. His father was waking up, immediately looking over his blackberry. He gave a cursory look at the world outside the car and raised his eyebrows while yawning at Karan.

'It's taking too much time.' That's all he said while shaking his head into his phone.

A Highway Deal

It was mid March when I visited the site in Ludhiana. As a contractor, I liked to visit the outstation sites at least once a month, and since this site meant a good deal of business to me, I visited it nearly every week.

I stood outside the new building for a few minutes, smoking a cigarette and recalling when this was a barren land – now two years on, it was to be Punjab's best mall. I entered with pride, the gleaming marble in the lobby reflecting the enormous atrium that rose majestically around me, towering sheets of glass with colourful banners proudly displaying the many important and celebrated brands that were entering the Punjab market for the first time.

My site manager, Prakash Negi, rushed towards me, bowing – his gesticulating movements unnecessarily exaggerated. Prakash Negi had been with my company for five years, by no means a long time for a family-owned company like ours, which had employees well into their thirtieth year. But his position was vital to the success of this project, indeed for the success of our company to make forays into the exciting Punjab state, nascent in its stages of expansion, rearing to explode and catch up with the southern states of our new, emerging India.

'Nearly complete,' I said, gesturing towards the polishing machines that churned on the marble, creating a whirl of swampy slush.

'Yes sir,' he exclaimed with pride.

We walked the site as I liked to do, traversing each floor, exploring every nook and cranny, corridors, lift lobbies, staircases, toilets, exit areas, everywhere.

I roamed the nearly empty corridors admiring our handiwork-neat coves in brightly painted ceilings and vitrified tile flooring with black speckled granite inserts. I looked proudly at the precise joints and patted Prakash on his back.

'Great job,' I said.

I entered the toilets, pointing out a crack in the mirror in the men's bathroom, the crack cutting a sparkling diagonal across my face, making an ordinary face look perversely handsome, although I was conscious of the grey streaks of hair around my temples and sides.

By the time we reached the seventh floor I was tired and my project manager's writing pad was full with instructions. I must start running again and drink less, I thought.

I continued, pointing out small quality issues, insisting that I was happy with the work, but that we could do that much better for it to be a perfect site. When I said, 'that much better', I joined my index and thumb fingers and squinted at him to make my point.

I smiled inwardly. A perfect site, a rarity in the chaotic world of contracting. Why did my extraordinarily pretty wife marry me? Thoughts of a perfect site and my perfect wife blended together.

On the cinema floor, the eighth floor, I was exhausted. We had been walking the site for over two hours and I had driven six hours in the morning from Delhi. I had driven fast and hummed to high school music that I had hardly heard after marriage, and barring a stop for a cola and a pee, I had driven non-stop. But I had also driven carefully, all too aware of the villagers who jumped out of nowhere, cows and dogs that meandered the roads as if it were a lush meadow.

That I would run over some hapless jay walker or animal, was a dread that I always harboured inside me. Each time I drove, I couldn't help but remember the various deaths that I had seen on the streets of Delhi and on the highways. The severed arm, the bloodied yellow sari, the crushed head in a helmet, the pieces of body parts smeared black and bloody against the tarmac, the decapitated heads, the lifeless infants splayed like dolls, the crushed bodies inside destroyed cars, the countless dogs with their intestines strewn like spaghetti – all these sights roamed my head viciously like a repulsive slide show of horror and tragedy.

There was training going on in the cinema foyer, the concession counter shone with bright lights and plasma displays, and the crack of popcorn and swish of coke dispensers lent gaiety to the site, lending a quick spring in the step of the few carpenters and painters that worked on minor touch-ups and improvements.

A cinema manager who recognized me walked towards me smiling broadly, bringing me a coke and popcorn.

'Congratulations sir,' he said to me, his uniform gleaming with stars and buttons. 'Welcome, welcome, this is your place!'

'Congratulations to you,' I said laughing. 'Thank you,' I added shyly.

Fictitious as his compliment was, I was glad for his large-heartedness. Compliments in my business were rare as diamonds and anything was greedily accepted.

After a few more polite compliment-exchanges that briefly keyed me out of my fatigue, he led me to one of the cinemas where the projector was being tested. I motioned Prakash Negi, who was happily munching popcorn by the fistfuls, to follow me. It was an old Shah Rukh Khan movie, I couldn't remember the name at the time, though months later the name suddenly came to me – *Baazigar*.

Grateful for the comfort of the velveteen seats, I watched a very young Shah Rukh Khan make his trademark expressions, and in the stirring, winding thoughts of school, old girlfriends, projects and my marriage, I fell asleep. When I awoke, the screen was blank, a mist of sparkles signalling the end of the spool. There was no one in the theatre. The projector created a funnel of light, dots of dust timidly darting in and out of its beam, the spotlight celebrating dust, dust that I must be inhaling now in the invisible space. Still lost in my stippled dreams, I breathed deeply to wake myself.

'You were fast asleep, sir,' said a smiling Prakash who was eating his ever full bucket, the gaps between his teeth mashed with popcorn.

I smiled back, hoping no popcorn embellished my teeth.

'Sir,' Prakash said nervously. 'Can I come back to Delhi with you? It is my wife's...'

I didn't wait for him to complete the sentence. 'Yes, you can, but please come back here after the weekend.'

'I will! I will!' he exclaimed happily. 'Thank you, sir.'

It wasn't the right time for Prakash Negi to leave the site even for a day. The site was weeks away from an ostentatious opening ceremony and many celebrities and politicians were expected to attend. But, I was thankful that he wanted to come to Delhi, I needed the company, and although I had driven to and from Ludhiana more than a score of times in the past year, I was weary and if sleep overcame me, Prakash Negi and I could drive in turns.

After a few more rapid instructions, and a hasty look around the terrace, we left Ludhiana at five pm. Dusk was an hour away, but the rush hour raced onto us and we were engulfed in the honking, impatient traffic at the edge of Ludhiana.

For an hour we hardly moved, the traffic situation further exacerbated by an overturned truck that lay on its side at the rim of the highway. It's black underbelly, and the red body from which spilled sacks of flour, snowy white powder like pus against the road, made the truck look like a giant cockroach. Everyone slowed down, craning and curious, at the sight of only a smashed windshield. There weren't any bodies to be seen, and everyone sped on, privately disappointed, as if the logjam would have been worth it at least at the sight of bodies and blood. Forgetting the accident in seconds, the stretch of highway enticed me towards its vanishing point.

Grateful to get out of the traffic snarl, I quickly sped the car up to hundred. I doubted we would be home before midnight.

Aware that my high school music, all English, rock and heavy metal, would hardly be appropriate or appreciated, I put on a popular Bollywood CD, one of my wife's current favourites. My wife loved all Bollywood movies.

I nodded cheerfully, as Prakash clicked his fingers, and although he was looking out of the window, I could see in the patches of reflection that he was mouthing the words contentedly.

The indigo sky sped away from us, receding into the ever-expanding horizon and the night caught up quickly. The yellow reflectors made an arrow in the middle of the highway. On both sides dancing shadows of tall eucalyptus trees wavered gracefully but spookily in the cool March air. I altered my speed between hundred and hundred and forty, slowing down only while overtaking, lurching the car into third gear and higher speeds in the empty stretches.

Prakash Negi was asleep and snoring, his hand clutching a bag of chips. His unfinished coke can rattled in the cup holder. I marvelled at his appetite and changed the music, turning the volume down, lest the beat of drums and streaking sound of electric guitar wake him up.

I had driven nearly four hours and was beginning to get sleepy myself. I could not wake up Prakash. He looked much too comfortable, his head resting on the seat belt strap, the chips now between his crossed legs, his face a picture of satisfaction and peace.

I didn't completely trust him, I thought, tapping my fingers on the steering to Green Day.

Early on there had been petty thefts at his sites that were attributed to him. It could never be proven and they remained just rumours. Over the years, he had gained the respect of the company, and had matured into a sensible, sharp and profitable project manager.

Still, there was something I found vaguely uncomfortable about him, like an over-zealous dog which could bare its teeth any time. His mannerisms were always dramatized, his respectful ways more theatrical than real. But I could find no fault in his work, and often the work on his sites surpassed others in quality and profitability alike. In that Prakash Negi was also the target of many a jealous snide remark. I cautioned myself against making pointlessly suspicious judgements.

Passing Kurukshetra, it was nearing ten pm. I had done well, I thought, with weary satisfaction.

The National Highway 1 curved in broad sweeps towards Panipat. The otherwise dark highway lit in patches as we passed small towns that fused readily, one into the other, almost an endless stream of towns.

My head felt heavy and I raised the volume of the stereo, rubbing spit into my eyes to keep myself awake. I concentrated on the reflectors and stayed in the middle of the road, wheels on both lanes.

I sped up to keep up my focus and adjusted myself in the seat.

I saw him, if only for less than a second. It was a figure dressed in white, a male, and I rammed my car into him at a speed of hundred and forty kilometres an hour. There was a shudder, a roaring crack, the sound of a headlight breaking, a grating sound in the underside of the car, and by the time I shrieked the car to a stop, a lifeless body was twenty metres behind me.

Prakash Negi woke up, shocked and startled out of his asleep.

I was trembling violently as I looked in the rear-view mirror. Prakash Negi turned his head and saw the body. The body was still. It seemed small, flat, and like a crumple of white sheets. Something lay detached from it several feet away. It seemed like an arm had been ripped off. Against the red brake lights of the car, I could see that the white kurta was quickly turning crimson, the colour was covering the whole body making it increasingly difficult to discern against the blackness of night and tarmac.

Prakash got out of the car quickly, his haste spilling the packet of chips. First, he checked the front of the car and then ran towards the body. He was back in less than a minute.

'He's dead sir. Let's go,' were his first words, distinct even against his panting breath. And they were calm and confident.

I didn't say anything. My eyes were fixed on the rear view mirror and my foot was on the brake. The road behind me was a motley of blacks and reds.

'Let's go, sir! There will be other cars here any second!' This time he raised his voice, nearly shouting at me.

I still did not move. 'We should wait... perhaps, hospital, the police....'

'Sir, he is dead. You have to move! You know what they will do to you! Move!'

I didn't move. I couldn't.

He wasted no further time. He got out of the car again, and ran towards the driver's side. He pushed me to the passenger side violently. The gear shaft caught me in my testicles, and the excruciating pain momentarily blanked out what had just happened.

He drove off just as we could make out headlights in the mirrors.

'Very lucky the road was deserted.' He spoke professionally, eerily, as if he had been through this before.

My blood began to run cold. I was terrorized, paralysed in action and words.

'Don't worry sir. This happens.' He patted my thigh. I suddenly realized that the stereo was still on. I switched it off. The quiet of the night swallowed me and I began to shake as tears spilled across my face and shirt in sobs of fits and starts.

Prakash continued to pat my thigh and kept telling me not to worry. 'He is dead,' he said repeatedly. 'Nothing would come out of your confession,' he reasoned matter-of-factly.

'You know what they would do to a man of your position?' he said. Without waiting for an answer, he continued, 'Make an example of you in every paper in the country. And then forget about you while your family pays lakhs, maybe crores, to get you out of a filthy jail.'

'There is no justice. Sir, the man is dead. Next time we will drive carefully.' He patted my arm. 'We have learnt from our mistake.'

The car was shaking slightly, the lone headlight marking out the road ineffectively.

'Is the car okay to drive all the way back?' I asked, my voice quavering.

He smiled and I saw a menacing, contemptuous twist in his smug expression and suddenly my grief and shock was overcome with fear, fear of Prakash Negi.

I fell asleep.

When I woke up, we were in Delhi, passing Pitampura, the TV tower a criss-cross of ghostly shadows against the cloudless, moonless night. It seemed as if it was a nightmare.

Prakash Negi had switched CDs and was once again humming the same popular Bollywood song. He seemed pleased with himself.

'Don't worry sir,' he said reading my mind. 'Think of it as a bad dream.'

'What if someone had noted down our car number?' I said in an automatic tone, sickened at my cowardice.

'No one did, sir. There was nobody around,' he said. 'Very lucky.' He nodded sagely.

'You can't be sure of that,' I said, this time in a more authoritative tone, adopting my more formal, stern position.

He raised his eyebrows and grinned at me. It was as if the devil was smiling at me. I ran my index finger around my gold kara feeling the cold grooves against my skin.

'No one knows sir. No one saw. Only I know. It is our secret.'

He continued, 'You can't take the car home. I will drop you home and I will take the car and get it fixed. It will be a matter of a few days.'

I didn't say anything. When we neared Sunder Nagar, where I lived, I asked him to stop the car before the colony gate. It was best that no one, including the private security at the gates, saw the car and me in this condition. I was sure that fright and guilt was writ large across my face.

'Please take comfort in the hot food that *bhabiji* will serve you.' After a slight pause, he confidently added, 'And later in her arms.' His eyes were wide with lust, his face triumphantly contorted.

I didn't say anything.

Hesitatingly, I said in a terrified low voice, 'Thank you.'

To that he nodded gently and smiled. As he drove off, he raised the volume of the stereo and I could almost hear the snap of his fingers.

My house seemed unfriendly and strange to me. My wife, Radhika, called out my name, to ascertain that it was me entering the house, and with the briefest of hellos, she busied herself to warm the dinner.

What had happened to us, I wondered, and with that very thought, the sight of the severed limb, the lifeless body, filled every corner of my mind like the blood spreading across the kurta.

I sat at the table as she set out mats, plates, other crockery and cutlery.

'How was work?' she asked, her back to me, thumbing digits on the microwave.

Before waiting for an answer, she continued, 'Why don't you wash up? You look very tired,' her voice was full of mechanical concern.

I had dinner while she watched me eat, dutifully filling my plate with more dal and sabzi, helping me to hot rotis. It was nearly one am.

She was wearing a thin negligee, the outline of her breasts easily visible in the shimmering kitchen light, and I felt an erection come hard and fast against my jeans.

When I pressed against her in bed, she smiled, her pink lips spreading generously across her fair face, her eyes limp with sadness.

'Not today,' she whispered, her diamond earrings sparkling in the darkness of the room.

We hadn't made love in six months. The last thoughts before I fell asleep, restless, erect and terrorized, were of the man I had killed, Prakash Negi hacking the body into smaller pieces, his smile engulfing Radhika inside his salivating mouth, swallowing her whole, her pretty ankles and beautiful feet dangling from clenched popcorn filled teeth.

'Where is your car?' Radhika asked the next morning, serving me toast, slightly burnt, just as I liked it, with a runny fried egg on top.

'Oh, Prakash and I drove back together. He dropped me first. I was too tired to drop him, it would have meant an extra half hour.'

The tea leaves were hissing. I wondered if she ever heard me anymore.

'Well, you can take my car. I don't have anywhere to go.'

I mumbled 'thank you', looked at the freshly garlanded photographs of my parents and left.

I took an autorickshaw and the guards at the Sunder Nagar gates looked curiously on. I had not ridden in an auto since school and the rushing air filled my ears, obliterating the clanging sounds of condemnation in my head, immediately evaporating tears that escaped from my eyes. In the bumpy, shaky ride to work, I felt slightly better. I tipped the auto driver a hundred extra rupees and as soon as I turned to enter my office, I saw a grinning Prakash Negi waiting at the gate. He was leaning against the boundary wall like a cowboy, lighting a cigarette just when he saw me, as if he had been impatiently waiting for me to arrive.

'Hello sir. Good morning,' he said politely. 'I hope you are feeling good?'

I tried to look blankly at him, attempting at masking my anger. He looked straight at me, and it was I who eventually averted my eyes.

He followed me in the office, into my cabin, but he stubbed out the cigarette at the reception.

'Let's get to the point sir,' he said. 'That's your favourite line, isn't it sir?'

'What the fuck do you want?' I said unable to control the rage that was building inside me, pressing against my chest and head with ferocity against this shit of a man who was clearly about to blackmail me.

'Five lakh a month,' he said pleasantly and without wasting a second. My expression changed to shock and fright. This was *actually* happening, I thought.

'Yes, I will be considered an accomplice if I go to the police.' He continued in his pleasant tone. 'But you are a rich man. I will say you coerced me into silence. The media will make a hero out of me for standing up to money and power.'

I couldn't believe what I was hearing. 'You have obviously thought this through.' I said. 'Very carefully.' My voice was shivering with every word and my eyes were blistering with tears.

He laughed loudly, a laughter that was certainly heard outside my cabin, a laughter that must have surprised all, since I was not one for frivolity and humour in the workplace.

'When I saw the body, yes, I began to think then. I looked at the severed leg, the crushed ribs protruding from his chest, the smashed face, the brain spillıng out of his ears and cheeks, the ripped abdomen...'

'Stop!' I screamed. 'Shut up!' I began wailing.

He quickly moved and locked the door.

'Now, you listen, you,' he paused, 'You have to compose yourself. This is your office. The people outside regard you as a God on Earth.'

'Don't fucking flatter me.' I said catching him by his collar, tears spilling on my arm.

He prised my fingers from his collar. 'Calm down. Forget what happened last night. It never did.'

'Just remember our deal, sir. All is well.' And with a gentle bow he left my room. Before the door clicked in place, I could hear him humming the Bollywood song from the previous night. It haunted me.

That evening and then every day for the next one year I wanted to confide in Radhika. I could not bear the guilt that terrorized my heart and numbed my mind. I wanted to tell her what had happened. Her father was a powerful lawyer. Maybe he could help me. I thought of all the political connections I had through friends of friends. I thought of everything.

I thought of killing him. I fantasized about contract killers with thick beards, stained yellow teeth and heavy gold chains. Then I would have killed two people, I thought.

Every day I waited for the police to barge in and arrest me. Every day I would imagine a barrage of media persons outside my house. It sickened me. It made me ill. The energy I had was weaning fast with each passing day.

Radhika would ask me, 'What is the matter?' and I would always reply, 'Nothing.'

She barely heard my reply. To her my mood must have been a mirror of our failing marriage.

In November she left me. She must have copied the scene from a movie because it was exactly like that. One evening I entered the house I had inherited from my parents, and instantly I knew it was empty. The servant, Ram, who had been with me since I was born, stood with a bowed head and crossed hands in front of the kitchen.

There was a note on the bed. It said, 'Take care.'

On the tenth of every month, I handed over five lakh, my bribe, the extortion, the protection money to Prakash Negi. Every month it was the same sequence.

He would come to the Sunder Nagar market to Sweets Corner, a place I had visited since childhood. It was the place where I had had my first crush, the place where I took my first girlfriend for our third date, the preceding two had been at fancier restaurants in five star hotels. It was where I had sat with high school friends, talking in loud tones wearing low slung jeans and beads around my neck. And now years later, the same waiters saluted a greying me, in cufflinks and pleats, a wealthy man, the shining tip of the Cartier pen matching the Cartier watch. They must admire me, I thought.

Prakash Negi would take the brown packet from my hand and touching it lightly to his forehead he would salute me. He would ask me to sit with him while he had chole bhatture. I had nothing, just sips of water from the mineral water bottle, not using the restaurant's glass that I thought was much too unhygienic.

He would chat amicably, tell me about his children and their schooling, and always call me 'sir'.

Since the accident and especially since Radhika left me, I was disinterested at work, keeping my phone switched off for days at end, preferring to switch channels in bed. Sometimes I roamed the monuments of Delhi, taking tours from government guides who I would tip ten times their fee, for their acknowledgement of bows and salutes. I bought the love of strangers. From waiters to valet drivers, I tipped them sums that they wouldn't earn in a week. Everywhere I went, I was treated like an invented king. I would have solitary meals talking to bartenders, who would laugh when I laughed, say yes or no, as was desired in my yearning, desperate expression.

At the company, the losses were mounting. There were hardly any projects in hand. People were getting restless and the company started emptying out. At first, the decline was slow, barely perceptible and suddenly it escalated, accelerating its own death.

One month, on the tenth, when the end of the company was imminent, I said to Prakash Negi, 'I want you to resign. You have enough money to start your own company. Take as many people as you can from here.'

He shook his head and laughed, but he didn't say anything.

'You will continue to get your money,' I said.

He looked at me with his menacing eyes, questioningly, as if the thought to discontinue had even crossed my mind.

He continued eating his chole bhature.

'I have set up a safe deposit box in Connaught Place. Every month on the tenth, you will find your money there,' I said quietly. I put on the table a few papers and a key.

When we said goodbye, I noticed it was the first time he didn't bow to me. There was a dance in his step as he walked away, as free of me as I was of him.

Nitin and I

Nitin and I had the time of our lives last night. The time of our lives in the life we remember anyway. We agreed on that. We saw Olivia Newton John dancing with the lead guy from *Crouching Tiger Hidden Dragon*. He danced like an idiot, but he flew around pretty good. We saw three Sylvester Stallones. They were dancing with each other, their veins popping on their foreheads and temples, their tight navy T-shirts boring deep into their eighteen-inch biceps. Then there was this girl in blue, unreal blue, wearing a dress which showed off her silicon tits and her legs that went on for miles. Right Said Fred.

We took rounds of her. Like she didn't know. The whole fucking club was taking rounds of her. There were geeks from Stanford who forgot their gin and tonics and stock market update and all the hedge fund crap, bending down to tie their shoelaces every time she walked past. Nitin and I didn't tie our shoelaces. But that's because we were wearing four hundred dollar loafers. The geeks grinned at us the way geeks grin. I told you so. I told you so. I told you what mother fucker, I wanted to scream. That we should have worn your cheap sixty dollar preppie shit you bastards! Just to see Under Her Skirt.

So we drank half sulking, watching Crouching zooming over our heads with Olivia trailing behind. She looked like she was having an orgasm. Or she was terrified to death. Or both. Crouching didn't care. He was doing flips now.

Meanwhile, Sly was hitting on Sly while the third Sly was getting jealous. He tried to get in between but got smacked in the face. The vein in his temple went off with a loud pop just when the music stopped for a second. No one noticed. Everyone thought it was part of the beat. The DJ was pissed off, the pause was meant to be dramatic. And Third Sly had spoilt it.

For a regular Thursday night, it was rocking like the Titanic. For a weeknight this seemed a bit unusual. A couple of thousands to the bartender revealed that nothing was ever regular here. So what would tomorrow night be like, I enquired. He smiled as he insisted on pouring a shot down our throats and said, 'Different.'

Suddenly we noticed Crouching getting into a huge row with Olivia. He beat the shit out of her. The shit apparently hit the boyfriend of the girl in unreal blue. We weren't as humored by the shit all over him as much as concerned about the fact that Unreal Blue had a boyfriend. Her boyfriend looked like Salman Khan. Or was it Saif? Perhaps it actually was one of them. Perhaps it wasn't. I didn't give a shit.

But whoever could trust a girl whose legs went on for miles? Salman Khan, I guessed.

Anyway, the boyfriend was so fucking drunk that he hit out at Crouching. Crouching, the health freak that he is, was the only person In the club not drinking and dodged everything with an ease that was equal to boredom. Then the boyfriend took out a gun and pulled the trigger ten times. Crouching caught five bullets in his teeth. His mouth was too full (he looked like a teenager with braces) to catch more bullets, so he somersaulted around the others. Three hit the ceiling and one ricocheted and hit Third Sly in the eye. Third Sly was mad with rage but someone quickly pulled out a compact mirror. Third was immediately ecstatic with his new look. He demanded some polish to shine his new bullet eye and a boy was sent to fetch some immediately. Two bullets hit us. One went right through my arm so that I could see through it. When I raised my arm to the strobe, light passed through the hole like an arrow. I was the object of sudden increased interest from some very young looking girls who formed a circle around me and danced wildly, bobbing their little tits as I shot arrows of light down at them which they ate, crunching the light noisily along with their Ecstasy tablets. Surprisingly, it didn't hurt all that much. The other bullet grazed Nitin on the right side of his jaw taking with it flesh and exposing a mottled grey bone. He looked a bit like Two-Face. Quite boring, really.

So we were Bullet-Hit-And-Survived-To-Tell-The-Tale. We enjoyed the attention. Third Sly too was showing off his bullet eye and promptly commanded greater respect from the other two.

But Crouching looked really mad in that Crouching Tiger Hidden Dragon kind of way – stony glistening eyes, flittering cheeks. Catching five bullets isn't easy and it took ten years of meditation under a peepal tree for him, during which he shat and pissed all over himself and became all skin and bones and nearly died to reach that level of enlightenment. But he decided to forgive Salman alias Saif in the name of world peace. He told me all this very quickly (with very bad breath) because I was standing nearest to him. His voice sounded like someone had pressed the fast forward button. The DJ added some beats and his story sounded like a rap song. The young girls with their little tits went mad with hip-hop excitement. I could almost see their deliciously pink nipples.

The boyfriend of Unreal Blue, Salman or Saif whichever it was, looked worried and upset. Rightly so. Crouching may have forgiven him but now Unreal Blue was dancing to Crouching's hip-hop on the bar and every man in the club was suddenly straining to get a drink. Nearly every woman looking cross-eyed and cross, standing with folded arms and upturned faces. Hurriedly they went to the ladies toilet to fix their makeup, outside which soon formed the Great Ladies Line. Nitin ordered the most expensive champagne that proved difficult to open. Eventually the cork flew out with rage and blasted into the crowd. Foaming gold sprayed everywhere. Some thirty seconds later an ugly fat chick was carried out by large bouncers, an errant Cock sticking out of the side of her head. Cork to Cock. Some metamorphosis, I thought. Chrysalis to Butterfly, I shrugged.

Unreal Blue was clearly impressed with the seven-hundred-dollar champagne; the size of a missile cradled in Nitin's arms, and angelically took the first sip. She churned it in her mouth before returning it back into Nitin's mouth following which a long slow kiss ensued.

I simply stood, sighed, raised my eyebrows and waited for the inevitable showdown. The Boyfriend and the Fight.

But with Crouching dying to try out his tenth dan super explosive finish-the-person-before-he-can-say-Crouchi – there was no way Nitin had to do anything. Crouching forgot about forgiveness and world peace. He gave a middle finger to Kashmir and he said to hell with Sudan. He spoke about all the wars in the world with such dizzying speed and rhapsody that the DJ gave up and went home.

Nitin watched, ate imaginary popcorn and kissed Unreal Blue intermittently while enjoying the show. The kisses got stronger and longer as the beating got more and more furious; the screams of the boyfriend (Salman or Saif) were a crescendo of agony and hit a pitch that only some creatures can hear. I can, I am born with dog-ears. If you were watching, you couldn't see Crouching's arms or legs, they were moving like the blades of a jet-liner, and there was a distinct whirr-whirr and everyone nearby was holding up their arms averting the Terrible Typhoon he was causing. Crouching's torso remained stationary, Buddha like, meditating in mid air while the limbs did their hacking.

Then what? Well, the typical third-rate come-fuck-me line that Nitin said to Unreal Blue, 'Will you come to my suite to have some coffee?' My suite. Wrong. On both counts. My. Suite. It wasn't his. It was ours. And I booked it so it was more mine. And it wasn't a suite. It was a standard room. But what pissed me off the most was the coffee line that took the hackneyed out of hackneyed.

But up they went, the gold-leaf elevator doors sliding together noiselessly, ending the night for me and beginning the night for Nitin. I wondered then whether Nitin and Unreal Blue would think of themselves as elevator doors, joining perfectly, becoming one. Later in life, when I made love to various women (four-hundred-and-thirty-six, but who's counting?), I would sometimes stifle a laugh thinking of elevator doors. Gold-Leaf Elevator Doors.

I went up and wrote this, most of it anyway, sitting outside the hotel room in the corridor, while Nitin could be heard making rude noises with Unreal Blue. He did come out once to hastily give me a tube of Pringles and a couple of Diet Cokes. I took a 'Please clean my room' sign from the opposite room and hung it on the door knob. Hugging my champagne and blood-soaked jacket close, I walked out to a dull morning. The sky was dotted with bored clouds yawning their way east towards an insipid rising sun. All that Sun God bullshit. Flagging a taxi, I told the driver to go the nearest hospital. It was time to get my arm fixed.

A Fine Provenance

When Siddharth Shah joined his art gallery, one of the first assignments was to go to London to evaluate a possible deal for an exceptional '70s Husain and an outstanding Benares by Ram Kumar, painted in the early nineties.

He was barely a year into the business and did not understand why his father insisted that he go and see the works in 'flesh'.

'It'll be a good learning experience, Sid,' he said. 'Besides, you have friends in London, don't you? I thought you would enjoy the trip as well.'

'Of course, Papa. But, this is an important decision. A million dollars' worth!'

'They certainly look good enough, excellent in fact, in these images.' He pushed the printed email towards Siddharth. 'But before making such an important decision, I want a family member to see their condition. In the flesh,' he elaborated, expansively spreading his arms.

'Besides, your sister is getting married next month and if I make this trip your mother will surely shoot me.' He didn't smile as he said it, but looked above the rim of his glasses, raising his eyebrows as he did so, his silver hair reflecting the lights that shone from the high ceiling in his office.

Mr Shah was a bulky man, everything about his frame seemed to flow from one mass to the other as if his appendages were sponged together with magical adhesives, but he was handsome, his features as clear as his limbs were not, his nose small, his eyes large and expressive for a man. His skin was cream coloured, and there was scarcely a hair on his smooth face, which he chose to shave only once a week. 'To sweep the shadow,' he said. His suits were all tailored from an old-fashioned shop in Connaught Place and Savile Row could have done no better. He liked to wear a cravat in the winters, and in the summers he wore bright silk pocket squares that accentuated the navy blazers he wore with khaki pants.

'All right Papa. Of course I'll go.'

'When do I leave?' Siddharth asked after a pause.

'Tonight.'

'Tonight?'

'Yes, tonight. Don't worry, I'll take Sunaina out.' He said playfully, referring to Siddharth's girlfriend of two years. Siddharth smiled back.

I love him so much, thought Siddharth.

He was glad his father liked Sunaina. He was thinking of proposing to her as early as next summer. By that time a year would have passed since her college graduation, a respectable time, and she would be twenty-three. It was much too young, he agreed, but he was sure she was the one he wanted to spend the rest of his life with. The thought that he pushed to a dark corner of his brain was that Sunaina had vowed not have sex till she was married.

'It's not you, Sid,' she cooed. 'It's just something I am against doing.'

'But, we do everything else.'

'Precisely.'

Of all his friends he was the only one who had not had sex yet, a fact that was not only known to all his male friends, but to practically everyone who knew him. He had confided in his best friend Nitin that he had not had sex yet and six months earlier on his birthday party in front of over a hundred people, a drunken Nitin had climbed on a rickety speaker and spoken into the mike, 'Happy Birthday Siddy! May you finally break open the locks of heaven and become a man!'

Those words didn't seem that distant to him as looked at his watch. He had to go home immediately and pack fast.

'Let me see these emails Dad, to go over the correspondence.'

His father passed the file to him, stubbed his cigarette, stood up and came around his oak desk. Siddharth bent down to touch his father's feet and his father clasped him by the shoulders, hugging his frail body, kissed him on his forehead and said, 'Love you Sid. Have a good time as well.' And with that he handed him a wad of pounds far more than was needed for a weekend trip.

When Siddharth protested, he waved him away with another strike of his match. All his friends found his father incredibly dashing. They adored him. It was true that his father had an aura of venerability that was evident to anyone. With a sigh of respect, he shut his father's cabin door, wondering if he would ever equal him in any manner.

In the flight on British Airways that took off exactly at two am, he was seated in business class, envious of the few that were in first and supercilious towards those that walked past to economy.

He read the correspondence between the seller, a Michael Smith, and his father. The first email, it was clear from its objective detachment, was a mass email. How many galleries could it have gone to, he thought. But the subsequent emails after his father's response of polite interest were considerably warmer in their tone, although they maintained a businesslike impassiveness about them. He looked at the images of the paintings. They were beautiful, large, oils on canvas, both superb representations of the earlier works of Ram Kumar and Maqbool Fida Husain.

It would be a trophy catch if they managed to seal the transaction. If I manage to seal it, he thought proudly as he sipped his third glass of vodka tonic, chomping on salted cashews and nuts. When he woke up, London was already on his right, the familiar sights of Tate Modern, the Eye, Canary Wharf, Big Ben, St Paul's Cathedral, and the skyline around the Thames inciting a familiar anticipation within him.

He was to meet Michael Smith at three thirty that afternoon. It is only six thirty in the morning, and he wondered how he should spend his morning. But as soon as he reached the hotel, he fell asleep, cosseted in the feathery softness of the giant beds, and erotic dreams of Sunaina.

Siddharth liked to be punctual like his father and after a twenty minute drive past flapping swans and lovers at St James Park, down Marylebone Road, he arrived at a cul-de-sac of apartments facing a corner of Regents Park. It was luxuriously elegant, a tuck of perfection in the heart of London. All the apartments were three storied, the numbers painted in gold on coffee coloured Corinthian columns, and black letterboxes at the entrance with the names of the owners in polished inlaid brass. Clearly these apartments didn't change hands very often, he thought. Large bay windows cantilevered from each floor supported by iron gargoyles, and the beautiful exposed brickwork of the building was painted only around the perimeters to match the coffee colour of the columns. Many of the entrances had large stone urns from which sprouted roses, peonies and pansies.

Mr Smith lived in 17B. After tipping the cab driver generously, to gain an approving smile from him, Siddharth skipped confidently towards the entrance and rang the white knob ingeniously placed inside the open mouth of a lion cast in bronze. The other two bells were also in the mouths of animals; 17A looked like a cross between a werewolf and a bird and 17C, the bell of the topmost apartment, had a friendly looking retriever. He noticed a small camera pointing straight at him, and as he looked up, Mr Smith buzzed him in.

He swung open a door made of wood, wrought iron and glass, and found himself in a plush hallway of black and white chess board flooring, a large console on one side of the hallway, and an elevator on the other. Beginning to get nervous he pressed 17B.

Stepping into the exact hallway as on the ground floor, he was greeted by a white panelled door on his left. Just as he was searching for the bell, the door opened, and a tall medium built man of pink complexion with the whitest of hair neatly combed down the left side greeted him with a large smile.

'Helllo Siddharth,' he said. 'My name is Michael Smith. Very pleased to meet you.'

'Hello sir,' said Siddharth stammering a little, 'Very very nice to meet you too.'

He must have been very handsome in his younger days, Siddharth thought, as he entered.

'My wife, Joanne.'

'Hello Ma'am.'

'Oh, hello, please call me Jo. Even my children do,' she twittered as she shook his hand warmly, taking an extra second as if sizing him up in a motherly way, already thinking of what to feed him.

'Thank you for having me Sir,' Siddharth said a little uncertainly.

'Call me Michael. Not Mike. And certainly not Sir,' said Michael Smith in an accent that sounded more American than British.

As though reading his mind, he said, 'Yes, I am American but I have lived here for twenty-three years. My accents are all mixed up, but I can't do a good Indian one!' He laughed and Siddharth nervously laughed with him.

They stood in a square lobby of indigo walls and white ceiling, the flooring of black and white chess board pattern continued inside, but in a circular kite pattern, the squares becoming smaller as they reached the centre, at which was a cast iron map of historic England, over which was a round, solid mahogany table which had scores of well-thumbed books on it. Several lay open. This is what this genial couple did, read through their hundreds of books that as Siddharth would discover, occupied every room bountifully.

Michael Smith led Siddharth to a small living room by the side of the lobby, the white panelled doors were ajar and magnificent natural light filled the room from the three bay windows that lined the length of the room. On each was an Indian style divan upholstered in brightly coloured Indian silks. The room looked like a small museum. There were

Chinese figures snarling from their porcelain forms, an Indonesian Buddha smiling benevolently, a massive lacquered Ganesha, a dancing bronze Natraja. A Calder mobile hung in one corner above an Eames chair, the patina of its underside a burnished gold. There were two Barcelona chairs, chocolate brown, the leather faded in the middle of the seat and the back, Marc Newson chairs in three colours that crowded around a Noguchi table on which was miniature Peruvian pottery. On the walls were calligraphic scrolls, swords of different shapes, Kabuki masks, a Warhol print, a Kitaj canvas, an early Picasso drawing, two Hockney watercolours and the sought after Husain and the Ram Kumar.

They seemed secure in their place there, happy to be honoured in the historic significance of the world of art around them.

'Here are the paintings, son,' he said.

Siddharth liked the sound of that – son. That was the first time anyone had called him son, and different from the Hindi *beta,* the word son sounding comforting and reassuring.

There was a large, three seat sofa in front of the paintings, and after calling out to his wife, Michael and Joanne Smith climbed on the sofa to bring the paintings closer.

'A better look for the boy,' he said.

Siddharth protested and tried to give a hand, but the sprightly Joanne lifted the paintings carefully from their space. It was evident that the paintings had hung there for a long period of time, for the wall behind was a faded yellow and charcoal where the frames had touched the otherwise bright cream walls.

'Seventy two by thirty two,' he said, pointing at the vertical Husain. 'Sixty by forty eight,' He said, pointing at the horizontal Ram Kumar.

Siddharth peered at the paintings as if examining them expertly, but he knew that they could tell as they stood together, their shoulders touching, smiling at him as they would to their own son, that he was no expert, no connoisseur of the arts, that he was just the son of an art dealer, an emissary for this afternoon, an agent for the deal.

After an uncomfortable pause, he stepped back and said in a reluctantly enthusiastic voice, 'Beautiful.'

'Aren't they,' said Michael cheerfully as a statement not a question. 'I'll be sorry to see them go.'

Siddharth shifted his weight from one foot to the other, his arms crossed about his chest, fidgeting, not knowing what to say, how to react.

'Thank you,' he said instead, to Michael and Joanne, looking from one to thc other with pursed lips and slightly raised eyebrows in what he hoped to convey an expression of solemn businesslike gratitude.

'Stay for a bit, won't you?' said Joanne. 'We hardly have company, it is nice to see someone so young interested in the arts.'

'I am sure the boy has better things to do. Girlfriends to meet,' Michael said with a twinkling wink and a lopsided smile.

'No, no,' he mumbled. 'Girlfriend is in Delhi.'

'Well, Joanne has some pastries, and she'll make us wonderful tea, though perhaps not as nice as the Assam and Darjeelings you are used to in India. Have a seat.' Michael said cheerily with perhaps a touch of melancholy about his tone.

They sat down on the Barcelona chairs while Joanne Smith happily busied herself in the kitchen.

'Son, do you want to confirm the purchase then? To your father?' He said the last question without any hint of condescension, just a kindly question to a boy forty years younger than him, a boy who looked uncertain in this overwhelming home, where history had gathered as easily as the light that poured in from an unusually blazing London sun.

'I'll do it later sir.'

'Michael,' he corrected him.

'I'll do it later, Michael.' They both laughed. Siddharth felt a wave of relief.

'We have a son about your age. And our daughter is a few years older. She is married.' He said proudly, 'And is expecting her second baby.'

'Congratulations,' said Siddharth.

Michael pulled out his wallet and showed him a photograph of a young girl, around six, smiling a gap toothed smile and waving from the photograph. 'My daughter's first child. Our first grandchild,' he said, and motioned his hand towards the kitchen when he said, 'our'.

'Congratulations,' repeated Siddharth.

'Thank you. They both live in the US. But, they will be visiting soon,' he said.

'That's nice. Do you see them often?'

'Not as often as I like, but more so this past year.'

Siddharth nodded.

'Well, I hope the paintings find a nice spot in your home, son,' Michael said.

He continued, 'I bought them directly from Husain and Ram Kumar when I visited India. We used to visit every few years.' He said, his arm waving again towards the kitchen, as if including Joanne in the conversation.

'I spoke to your father on the phone. He assured me that he would not sell these paintings,'

Siddharth was surprised hearing this. His father had told him nothing of any telephone conversation.

He continued, 'Everything here has been collected with such pleasure.' He pointed at the Kitaj canvas 'We didn't know how much that would be worth one day.'

'Or any of this,' he said sweeping his hands about the room.

'Your...' he stopped himself. 'Joanne, just loved to collect everything she could lay her hands on when we travelled. We went with one suitcase but came back with six.' He laughed, his blue eyes glowing as he spoke.

'Well, I hope they find a nice home in your home,' he said.

'They definitely will,' Siddharth said nervously, shaking his head from side to side.

'It's important for Joanne and me to take care of all our affairs now. She wants me to dispose of all the art that can fetch good value so that we distribute the sums between Thomas and Leah.'

'My son and daughter,' he added. Siddharth nodded.

He sighed deeply. His face wasn't as wrinkled as could be clichéd of old people, rather it was quite smooth, a few crevices around his eyes and lips that deepened when he smiled.

Siddharth could hear cupboards opening and closing, the simmer of water boiling, the nimble steps of Joanne about in the kitchen.

'I should go help,' he said and stood up.

Michael smiled, 'I think she would like that.'

Siddharth entered the kitchen, a kitchen much smaller than his in Delhi, but a kitchen from a children's book. It was U shaped, as if hugging you within it, an enchanting place to cook and eat, to sip wine, to furnish the body with nourishment and health, gaiety and laughter. The island in the middle had neat bowls of fruit and bread, and above it hung an assortment of pots and pans, some in shapes he would have thought impossible. Five chairs in an aquamarine blue were placed around it, the lathe turned legs had hand painted flowers on them that matched the print on the ivory cushions, tied with dried wheat stems. The exposed brickwork was laid as in an Italian pizzeria, but little could be seen of it, for hung in every available space, were collections of bells, masks, and family photographs. The Spanish limestone flooring was laid in broad tiles, the edges chamfered, and in front of the stove the flooring had the softest indentation where Joanne Smith had stood and cooked many times.

And she stood there now, her broad back to Siddharth, her apron tied in a firm knot, her skirt flaring from underneath, the tortuous cavalcade of sapphire varicose veins on her calves like the tributaries of a river.

'May I help please?'

'Oh, thank you,' she said turning around, not in surprise, as if she knew he was standing there all along.

But there was nothing really left to do for Siddharth as the cups and saucers were already laid neatly on a tray made from slats of dried banana leaves.

She deftly scooped up hot pastries from the stove and placed them on a large oval plate. 'It's nice for Michael,' she said, motioning her arm towards the living room when she said his name, 'That these paintings are returning to India.'

Siddarth nodded vigorously.

'Your father was such a gentleman on the phone. So understanding. Without having met us at all!' she said, her tone rising in grateful appreciation.

She sighed, a bouquet of tears gathering in her grey eyes, 'I just want him to live these last months at peace.'

Siddarth's shoulders flinched. She noticed the change about his eyes, his eyes full of fear and apprehension.

'Oh,' she said. 'Oh,' she said again. 'You didn't know.'

'I, I...' Siddarth stammered.

'He's dying of cancer, its everywhere' she said, once again motioning towards the living room.

'Your father must have thought it best for you not to know.' She nodded with gracious sympathy.

'At such a young age, you are,' she continued. 'Probably best not to deal with the business of death and just deal with business.' She said it laughingly, but with a touch of pity.

'We thought you would know. Forgive us,' she said. 'But we won't mention any of this to Michael. He seems to like you. He doesn't ask people to stay, you know.' She said it with quick nods as if agreeing with herself.

'We agreed to stop all treatment two months ago. The people at the hospice are very understanding, very kind indeed. Michael and I like them. But he would like to die at home, surrounded with his art, and if he's lucky, around family.' She said pointing at Thomas and Leah smiling from the many photographs.

'Come,' she said, 'let's join him. He can't bear to be alone.' And as she said it, Michael called out to her in endearment, 'Darling.'

Siddarth picked up the tray, his hands were quivering, and looking down at the steaming pastries he thought he had never called Sunaina that. She was just 'baby', and perhaps she *was* a baby. And probably so was he. Why didn't Papa tell me about Michael? Am I too young as Joanne had said, he thought in distressed wonder.

They joined Michael and soon the three of them were munching on the home-made pastries that made crunchy sounds as they melted easily in the mouth. The tea was delicious, supple with spices, the best he had ever had.

'So, tell me about your lady at home,' said Michael between bites, wiping his mouth carefully.

'Her name is Sunaina,' said Siddarth.

'Do you love her, son?'

'Michael!' said Joanne. 'How can you ask? We've barely met the boy,' she exclaimed.

'No, no, it's all right,' Siddarth said. 'I think so,' he added mechanically.

Michael nodded. 'You be honest with yourself son,' he exclaimed, but his voice dropped suddenly and he took a deep breath. 'You be honest with your girl.'

Joanne patted Michael's knee, 'You must rest.'

Michael nodded, the brightness in his blue eyes weakening.

'I should go,' said Siddarth. 'Please rest Michael.' When he said his name he felt an ache in the inside of his chest that tugged at his throat.

'Please finish your tea,' Michael said, his back resting on the cool leather, his wife's hand stroking his knee. They finished their tea in silence.

At the door, Siddarth thanked them profusely, the customary sentences of gratitude escaping lips from which he wanted to say much more.

They smiled kindly at him. Michael said, 'Please thank your father from us. Joanne will ship the paintings as soon as, well, you know. Till then, I will enjoy them.'

'Goodbye son,' he said closing the door gently.

A Contract of Dreams

I woke up in the morning, my stomach throbbing, my wrists smelling of a woman's expensive perfume, my mouth stinking of last night's tequila. It was already ten. I was late for a meeting.

The mist before my eyes did not lift and the headache only got worse when I jumped in the icy shower. I tried to throw up the remnants of last night. It made a swirling pink pool of rice and alcohol around and in my toes before angrily emptying down the drain.

Shaking my head, I got ready quickly, gulping down a cold glass of milk that churned in my stomach as I sat in the car instructing my driver to head to Greater Noida. I kissed the Hanuman pendant on my chain and thanked god that the meeting was far and that it would take me at least an hour to reach. I instantly passed out as the car crawled slowly through the morning Delhi traffic.

I woke up about fifteen minutes away from my meeting point. This was the second negotiation meeting and I knew that my company desperately needed the contract. The client wanted a large hospital to be built on the Greater Noida Expressway and although the first negotiation had been tough, as all negotiations in my line of work always are, I knew we had a good chance.

I popped down the sunshade to examine my eyes. They were bloodshot and my mouth stank with every breath. My driver said, 'Sir, drink smell.' Before I could react to his brazen remark, he had already parked the car on the side near a *paan-walla* and quickly got me a host of mouth fresheners. I accepted them gratefully and grudgingly. Worried, anxious, hung-over and tired, I popped half a dozen in my mouth till my mouth steamed with mint and tequila. I wanted to throw up again.

The project director at my company, Mr Rathore, was pacing the road outside the client's head office adjacent to the hospital plot. He was smoking with a smirk on his face. I got out, aware of my unsteady feet, aware of his scorn, aware of my stinking breath and my unqualified presence.

I am a civil contractor, I repeated to myself as I shook hands firmly with him. Rathore raised his eyebrow and said, 'Late night?'

I nodded, hating him, hating the way he asked me questions in his patronising, superior tone.

'Have this,' he said handing me a paan masala packet. 'The smell will go away.'

I took it with downcast eyes, tore it open and smacked down all the contents, chomping down hard into the bitter-sweet rocks, my jaws hurting, my eyes watering with embarrassment, shame and fear.

Rathore had already filled out our details at the security point and we were escorted into an empty conference room. It was large but not well appointed. The panelling on the wall was laminate, not veneer, the ceiling was cracked and it had undulations, the coves were badly edged, the lighting was too strong, the white board was of cheap quality and the flooring was low-grade Rajnagar marble stained with blackened joints.

Our earlier meeting had been at the architect's office. Clearly, we would be meeting the owner today.

As if reading my mind, Rathore said, 'I have heard Sanghvi will be here for this meeting.'

He sneered at me as he said this and I continued biting down on the paan masala, the red dust filling my mouth, the small pieces sticking between my teeth.

I took my seat, allowing Rathore to sit on the first seat next to the head of the table, hoping the client would not smell my stinking breath or notice the red eyes.

I wished I had remembered to put Vizine in my eyes. Fuck, I thought.

The door opened and in walked the head architect and her assistant. From the project management company there was a senior partner. From the client's side there were the purchase director, the accounts director and the owner, Mr Sanghvi.

In my last meeting I had met everyone but Mr Sanghvi. I had been expressive and earnest. I had even surprised Rathore by gently pointing out the aberrations in the drawings. I had spoken with confidence, negotiating hard on the payment terms.

For my effort then, I had received a condescending pat on my shoulder from Rathore's heavy hand. My ears had burned, my eyes had glazed over with gratefulness.

But today was different. I clicked my ankles hard under the table and got up to shake hands. The architect and the owner held my gaze for an unnecessary and uncomfortable second. They knew, I thought painfully.

Mr Sanghvi was in his mid fifties with a white goatee and salt-and-pepper hair that stuck out in all directions like a porcupine. He was much too fair and the skin on his face was soft and loose. He spoke authoritatively and commandingly in a tone more patronising than Rathore's and looked impassively at each one of us as he spoke in sentences that were long, full of punctuated, uncomfortable pauses.

He was enjoying this and I could only look back gloomily with reddened eyes, careful to focus on the tip of the Mont Blanc pen that peeked from his shirt pocket.

'Mr Kapoor, young man, how old are you?'

'Twenty-six,' I replied, unsteady and uncertain.

'I like young blood,' he said.

He said it like he wanted to have a taste of me. I waited for him to continue, till I realized he expected me to say something. I mumbled an unsure and unconvinced, 'Thank you.'

The architect cleared her throat.

I felt all eyes on me, like a specimen in a petri dish. Paan paraag was uncomfortably lodged somewhere around my front teeth and

I rubbed at my upper lip hoping it looked like a grave and mature gesture, at the same time keeping my breath in check.

'Your father, what's his name? Hemant? Why didn't he come?'

'He's retired sir. I...' motioning to Rathore. 'We look after things.'

He looked sceptically at me. He looked doubtfully at Mr Rathore.

'So, you want to do this project. Your quote is not good enough. Are you technically qualified?'

My eyes darted to Rathore, begging him to intervene, but he just sat there, his own hand on his upper lip, mimicking my gesture, smiling contemptuously. His arrogance was grating on my jangled nerves. He knew how important this contract was for us. The company had reached a critical point and we had to get at least ten crores of work or else we would begin losing money in two months. This job was worth fifteen crores and it would guarantee us months of safety, not to mention peace. The office was already in near uproar. Our suppliers and contractors were making daily visits to the head office, demanding their outstanding payments. Many were threatening legal action, some were even resorting to verbal abuse.

I tried to keep my expression neutral. I answered, 'No sir, I am not technical, but with the help of colleagues like Mr Rathore who is like a partner in our company, I have learnt much. And I continue to learn. I promise that if given the chance we will do our best. As for the price...'

'Your price is not good enough,' he interrupted. A nervous silence filled the room.

The architect cleared her throat again.

The project management partner, Sanjay Luthra said, 'Kunal, the price is not competitive. There are three other contractors and your quotation is the highest. Not by a small margin but by, let's see 15, no, 20 per cent.'

'Wow,' I mumbled.

'Yes, wow,' he reiterated. He was well into his fifties and his bald head glistened with sweat even though the room was cool.

The hair that he swept across his baldness stuck like thickened charcoal across his scalp.

At this point Rathore tapped his pen arrogantly on the table. I was immediately embarrassed, but I knew he would not let a project management representative, all of whom he thought of as lazy, incompetent, theoretical and highly paid idiots, to have the last word. After five years at my company, my opinion of project management companies was as disdainful if not as vociferous towards their employees.

'Mr Sanjay', Rathore said, 'the price is final. If you want a 2-3 per cent discount as a goodwill gesture, we can happily offer that. But, no more than that. This 20 per cent difference is not possible.'

'Mr Arvind Rathore, I can show you the papers,'said Sanjay, pushing the paper towards us in a mocking, menacing gesture. He looked helplessly at the owner.

They continued to argue and I looked up at the bright lights glaring angrily down at me from the ceiling that was much too low and shabbily painted. My eyes reddened further and brimmed with tears.

Six years ago, after my graduation from a second-grade business school in Delhi, I had timidly approached my father, begging him to let me study to be a film director.

My father, Hemant Kumar Rastogi, was a self-made man. I hated those words: 'Self-made'.

I heard it from my father at every opportunity but especially after the two drinks he had every evening and especially when we sat in his Mercedes, his hand softly caressing the calf leather.

Each time, he began by saying, 'At your age, I could not even imagine that I would one day own a car like this.' His eyes flashed with arrogance, his lips spread with conceit, the haughty smile making his face hideous. I would nod with false acquiesce like a dog, and I would continue my automatic nodding as he spoke of how the hundred rupees in his pocket turned into a five-hundred crore company. It seemed like each time he told his story, it was a validation of his life, and each time the story ended with the same moral – that I was lucky, unbelievably lucky to be his son, and that as his son I had got everything on a platter, the chance to head this company, the chance to make five hundred into a thousand. Two thousand. Five thousand. Ten thousand.

I had told him at the age of eleven that I wanted to make movies and laughingly and indulgently he had bought me my first still camera, a Leica M6. I instantly fell in love with it – the cool metallic frame, the crinkled leather, the quiet confident sound of the click. When I fell in love for the first time exactly a year later, and felt the softness of an uncertain hand in mine, I was reminded of my camera and the uncertainty with which I had held it. I had smiled into her trembling eyes, holding her hand with delicate firmness, my own heart trembling, waiting expectantly until her fingers laced around mine.

As the year went by the camera began to slip into my fingers like second nature and I clicked everything. In that year I took over five thousand photographs

The photographs covered the walls of my room from ceiling to floor. Landscapes, people, portraits, paintings, objects, animals, almost every imaginable shot was there. Laughter, annoyance, women pumping water (it was always women), crying children, lovers in parks, football games (never cricket), funeral processions, snarling dogs, weeping men (it was always the men who wept), brooding servants, unhappy businessmen, bored artists, defeated writers, brokers smoking outside the Delhi Stock Exchange, lonely men, busy prostitutes. I managed a lot.

I was young but I was rich. I had a driver and a car and I generously tipped my driver to take me to the many desultory corners of Delhi. If we were found out in these corners, he would be fired, I would be punished and my camera would be taken away. But, it was a mutually beneficial relationship for my driver and me, and it was these seeds of the early days of blackmail and bribery that gave my driver the audacity, or at least the coolness to tell me that my breath was stinking of alcohol. He used the word 'sir' now instead of 'baba', but I was still a child to him. A child whose dreams were violated, demolished and laughed at.

Oblivious to the fire that burned in my eyes, my parents didn't care about my obsession. My mother brought her kitty party friends conceitedly to my room to show them my talent. But it was a flippant show. They never heard the passion in my voice when I spoke about film, instead they laughingly and dismissively remarked that my voice was breaking and that I was becoming a man. Finally. Finally, becoming a man. My father would boast to his friends with their burgeoning collections of cars and single malt and their white hairy chests that he would soon take his fourteen-year old to his construction sites. And he did.

I was in awe. I was in awe of the unfinished structures, wide-eyed, even as I was distracted by the colourful abuses my father rained at his project managers, of the downcast expression they had on their face, at the way they smiled adoringly when my father threw a word of praise at them like throwing loose change at a beggar. I was in awe of the children that played daringly close to the precipice of the top floors, of their mothers burning the *choolah*, wiping bursts of sweat with the palloo of their sarees, many of them pregnant with a fourth, perhaps fifth child, of the fifty-year-old labourers with their sinewy arms and their abdomens cut like soft butter, of the young boys and their untidy underarms as they carried impossible loads on their heads, of the torn trousers and the red underwear that peaked out unashamedly through their fly, at the way they rolled up their vests above their nipples, exposing perfect bodies streaked with dust and shining sweat, of the way the mothers breastfed their infants in cool corners and against glistening concrete columns, of the scaffolding that looked like a cage on which men swung like monkeys a hundred feet above ground without harness or helmet, of the yawning excavations in which trucks looked like toys, of the sparks that flew from a welder's rod, of the sound that cutting machines made against wood and stone and the searing straight lines that shot from underneath the diamond-edged tools.

I was in awe that many touched my father's feet when he walked the site. I was in awe that here a human was not a human but simply a tool.

I took every conceivable photograph at the sites and plastered them on my ceiling. At night I lay in bed staring at them and the ceiling looked like a construction site, the corners of the photographs curled, exposing star-shaped patches of white ceiling. To me, it was the night sky.

Rathore was nudging me. I blinked and looked at him. My head was suddenly clear and I knew my eyes were no longer bloodshot. He was glaring at me. I had probably missed a minute of the meeting. Mr Sanghvi was in muted conversation with his accounts director. Mr Sanjay Luthra also stared at me while the architect looked amusingly on. I knew I could fuck her if I tried. She was in her early thirties; the v cut of her green kurta, probably from Fabindia, exposed the telling shadow of her small breasts. She wore glasses much too large for her face. She was not pretty but her lips were soft and her perfect ears could be gently licked. I returned her amused look, and excused myself to the toilet.

The toilet was a shabby job. Cheap tiles lined the walls, their joints scarred with uneven white grout as if laid by a blind mason. The mirror was peeling and the ceiling had the same white lights untidily inserted in it. I smirked.

The sanitary balls clinked as dark urine splashed on them. I was still dehydrated. We had to get this project, I thought. The meeting wasn't going too well. I wondered if the fact that I was not an engineer would be a moot point. I shook my head nervously. I had been naive in school, dreaming of an impossible future. I should have worked to become an engineer. Towards the certain future that had been planned for me.

Wallowing in naivety, for me making film was always the obvious choice, the line of work I wanted to pursue. For my father, his son would never have the mentality to be an engineer; but not taking over the family business was never a consideration.

It was one evening after my graduation that the realization of this acute discrepancy shocked me out of my gullibility.

'Dad, I want to learn film making,' I said. 'I would like to go to Bombay, there is a course, a private course, but it's very good.'

'We have three sites in Bombay. You'll learn well on the sites. See the projects,' he said, hardly looking away from the evening news on television.

'But Dad, this course is a full-time course and...'

'Kunal, this childhood hobby of yours is exactly that. Your childhood is speaking now. Think of more mature things. You have had a party for these three years. It is time you started working and took on responsibility. I have worked for thirty-five years.'

'But Dad, what I really want to do is...'

'Kunal! Enough! Are you not grateful to God for what you have!'

Of course, he meant that I was not grateful to him.

I had spent the last three years of college barely attending a single class, instead bribing the college clerks to clear my attendance, choosing to spend my days clicking photographs, smoking joints and drinking heavily. Those three years are a distant blur, almost as if they never happened. The impermanence of girlfriends who posed for me, some in the nude, the urgent sex I had with them, the languishing attitude of passing best friends, and as unreal and transient as it was, it was the only reality that gave me happiness in an otherwise frustrated existence.

Shaking my penis of the last drops of coagulated urine, I zipped my trousers, washed my mouth clean of the little rocks, pulled a string from a dirty towel, flossed my teeth quickly and made my hair so that a part of it swung sexily on my forehead. I should fuck that architect, I thought as I made my way out of the door.

The conference room was empty. I called Rathore from my mobile. He said that they had walked over to the site, the empty plot for the hospital.

When I began to say I would join them, he interrupted and said in a low voice, 'Kunal, we have a chance. See what you can.' It was an order. I knew immediately what he meant.

Unruffled and armed with the alcohol that swam in my passionless blood, I walked quickly across the table to Sanjay Luthra's empty seat. The file was open. I scanned the figures.

The bastard, I thought. Our quotation was the lowest. The job was ours. It had to be, I thought gleefully.

I immediately thought of the pride I would see on my father's face when I would tell him. I thought of the Macallan 18 years that he would offer me. I called Rathore and told him what I had seen.

'Come to the site.'

Ambling out with confidence and flossed teeth, I walked to the site. I strayed near the owner and asked for a minute of his time alone. He motioned to the others to carry on back to the office.

I looked at him with genuine sincerity and said that my price was final but for him I would offer a 3 per cent discount. I said that I would do my best, my company would do its best and that I would personally visit the site often. I was cautious not to specify what often meant. I knew clients always remembered these words.

I could see he was impressed with my confidence. I could see that I had won the job. We walked back to the conference room, and he asked me and Rathore to wait outside.

When they called us in, Mr Sanghvi looked at me and at Rathore and said, 'Ten percent discount and I am willing to give you the chance.'

He continued, 'I have not asked the other contractors to give their final price. Undoubtedly their price would go further down increasing the difference. This is a good chance for you.'

When he said 'you' he looked directly at me, his white goatee covering his condescending smile but the condescension still visible in his raised eyebrows and in the twirl of his Mont Blanc.

'Six per cent, sir,' I said. 'And that's final. Please sir.'

I was begging.

Rathore glared at me.

'Eight, Kunal,' he stood up and offered his hand.

I stood up as well.

His outstretched hand trembled, undoubtedly exhilarated at the deal he was getting. I shook it. Rathore looked on glaring, shaking his head at me.

Later outside their office, standing at the exact spot where we had met three hours earlier he said while puffing angrily at his cigarette, 'Doesn't matter. I'll make it up. Doesn't matter that you got carried away. I'll make it up. We'll have to get cheaper labour. You saw the quality in their office. They won't expect too much. I'll make it up.' He was talking to himself and I was barely listening.

He offered to drive together to our office. I politely declined.

Sitting in my car, ignoring his obtrusive expression, I slammed the door shut. Driving down the Greater Noida Expressway, I imagined my car from a camera in a helicopter. I imagined the swirling shot of my car zooming outwards further and further away as the lens panned up to an endless clear blue sky. I smiled. I told my driver to take me to the movies.

The House

When Gautam Khurana asked Prateek Kapoor to construct his farmhouse, Prateek was reluctant.

He didn't like working with friends and Gautam and Prateek had been friends since high school. House contracts were always complicated, involving too much direct interaction, which would mean that he would be spending much time talking business with Gautam.

But Gautam Khurana was a rich man who was spending tens of crores on his new house and the contract would have a significant impact on Prateek Kapoor's finances and fortunes. Besides, Gautam's house would surpass any hotel in the city, which would mean miles of mileage in high society, a society that enchanted him, a society he hungered for and hankered to be in, licking his lips looking at the society pages in newspapers every morning, combing tabloids with slavering attention.

On a Wednesday afternoon, with thoughts of grandiosity and imaginings of flamboyant press articles, Prateek agreed to let himself be coaxed into taking the job. He knew his wife Megha would be happy. And that made him feel happy, but a little sad as well. Megha always compared themselves to Gautam and Priya, Gautam's wife.

But he tucked away the sadness deep in his armpit, thinking of the wide smile he would get from her, the soft kisses, the chocolate she would feed him with her slender hands and later from her mouth.

When he entered his Panchsheel house, an exposed brick structure of modest size, elegant and comfortable, it suddenly felt small, compared to the forty-thousand-square-foot mansion he would be building for Gautam Khurana. He took off his shoes as he always did at the threshold and touched the feet of the huge Ganesha statue painted in greens and golds in the double-height lobby.

'I took Gautam's contract.' He told Megha, who was making salad in the kitchen. The cook and the maid hovered like bees around her.

She flung her arms about him and gave him a big kiss. 'Congratulations, Prat darling! Gauti can get no one better than you. You're the best.' She ordinarily would have not kissed or hugged him in front of the cook and the maid, reserving her affections for the confines of their bedroom.

He hated it when she called him 'Prat' and hated it even more when she called Gautam 'Gauti'. Only Priya called Gautam that, but Megha would only call Gautam by his nickname and sometimes it seemed especially and purposefully in front of Priya. It would embarrass Prateek and he would look down, change the subject or simply excuse himself to the bathroom because he was sure that Priya could tell of his discomfited fidgetiness.

'So, tell me about the house,' she said, her mouth full of salad, making crackling sounds.

Prateek had already told her a dozen times about the new Khurana house. The thousand-square-foot puja room made entirely of Thosis marble, the beauty salon, the massage rooms, the three-thousand-square-foot bedrooms, the hundred-thousand-dollar wardrobes, rain showers the size of coffee tables, single malt and cigar rooms, dining room to seat twenty, indoor and outdoor pools and the contemplation of a helipad.

So he told her again. As he talked, this time more patiently, he looked at his wife's throat move as she swallowed, at the cream skin curving with infinite gentleness towards her perfect breasts. By the time he had finished telling her, he wanted to make love to Megha, telling her every detail, taking her through every room, as if in virtual reality, her eyes dreamy and distant, his desperate and longing, and he felt like he would explode.

Refusing food, he took her up to their bedroom, and made love to her as gently and patiently as he had told her about Gautam's house, and when he finally came inside her, he saw a reflection of Gautam in her eyes. But true to his prediction, she reached for her side table drawer and brought out chocolate and fed him with her slender hands, and then teasingly put a piece in her mouth.

He felt repulsed and his primal need urged him to fight, and as he took the chocolate from her mouth into his own, he fought the Gautam in her eyes, the Gautam, richer, successful, and more handsome, the Gautam who could play every sport, the Gautam who laughed plenty, the Gautam to whom he could never measure up.

When they lay in bed in characteristic fashion later, Megha smoking, Prateek disgusted by the smoke and himself, she said, 'So, when does work start?'

'Monday,' he replied monotonously.

She looked at him sharply, her eyes screwing up at his tone.

He quickly added, 'Priya and Gautam have invited us to celebrate on Saturday.'

At that she fell asleep contentedly, her back to him, and he leaned in to spoon against her. She locked his ankles in hers.

At least she's mine, he thought.

With that he fell asleep into the most disturbing of dreams in which Gautam took the shape of a tornado, his handsome face threateningly laughing at him, scooping up Megha in the dust of diamonds that rushed around him at the speed of light.

'To us,' toasted Gautam on Saturday night as he raised his glass.

Prateek, Megha and Priya stood in a semi-circle, as if worshipping him, and they mimicked his actions and chorused after him.

'Hmmm,' said Megha, 'amazing wine. What is it?'

When she said 'amazing', she stressed on the word, elongating it.

'Opus One darling,' said Gautam putting his arm around Megha's shoulder, his fingers clearly on her bra strap. He looked down at her with a brilliant smile, pausing in step and sentence, while she giggled back at him girlishly.

Priya and Prateek pretended as if nothing had happened, because indeed nothing had, but it was enough for them to feel a press against their hearts, hearts that were already fragile, hearts that were on the brink of a fracture. Opus one flowed into whiskey, cigars and brandy and by the time Megha and Prateek left, the four of them were drunk, their thoughts adrift in deep waters sailing through dreams and ambitions.

Work at the site started on Monday, as Prateek had decided.

In a few months, Prateek comfortably eased into the project. He was exceptionally diligent with the work on Gautam's site, careful with quality, adhering to a project plan that didn't allow for mistakes. The basement was done and the ground floor columns stood ready to receive the slab casting. He was ahead of schedule. More than relief, he felt vindicated. It felt like he had two clients for this project, Gautam and Megha. While it was obvious to report site conditions and progress to Gautam, he would feel sullen and resentful when Megha asked him about the site, which was every evening.

One afternoon Prateek stood at the site, his shirt sleeves rolled up, sweat making crescents in his armpits, his eyes squinting at the concrete shimmering like a mirror. It was lunch break and the workers ate in the shade of trees and cement bags, immediately rolling over after to sleep, their faces pressed against their arms, their backs to the unrelenting sun.

He stood there in contemplation, his shadow long against the white earth, when he noticed another shadow appear.

It was Priya. He knew before he turned around.

'Hello Prateek,' she said.

'Hello Priya,' he said, smiling, conscious of his sweat streaked shirt, his smell of sweat, dust and concrete.

'This is the first time I have come to the site,' she said.

Prateek nodded.

She continued, 'It'll be time to start interiors soon, and Gauti thinks I should begin to get involved.'

When she said her husband's name, her voice dropped a note in reverence. Prateek nodded again and he said in a low voice, 'Absolutely,' keeping his arms stiff against his body so that she would not notice the sweat puddles.

She circled the site before going in as if it were an animal that might leap out at her. When she entered the threshold, she stepped gingerly as she did as a new bride, entering Gautam's Golf Links house on their wedding day.

This day, it seemed strange but wonderfully liberating that she was entering this house for the first time not with her husband but with another man. An improper thought and she shook her head in quick movements.

Prateek, watchful not to patronise, explained to her the various rooms. She looked gloomy and discontent. When he took her to what would be Gautam's and her bedroom, she stood in the middle, looking lost and tiny in the vast empty expanse that stretched around her, a room that would later be embellished and adorned with furniture from France and Italy. He stood at the doorway watching her, a light breeze beginning to sway her dress, the shade of the site and the cool plastered walls a welcome relief from the merciless heat outside.

'It's enormous,' she said.

'You are a big family,' he said referring to Gautam's parents and two younger brothers.

She nodded. He too nodded back. They didn't know what to say.

She smiled at him. It was the first time they were alone since he had known her.

They were aware of it. They shifted from one foot to the other. The anchor of Gautam's presence was missing. Fear, caution and freedom spread in their shadows. When they stepped outside, he saw the workers looking at her, her white dress perfectly still again, a spotless aberration, a mirage in the fiery earth. He felt protective towards her, as if he should put his arm around her shoulder.

Priya put on her large sunglasses, looked at him for a few seconds, before the chauffeur shut the door of her car. He stood there looking at his own reflection in the darkened window unsure if she was looking at him.

Gautam called him up a week later, his voice more animated than usual.

'Priya is going to Bombay for a friend's wedding. Saturday night, my place. Boy's only.'

With that he hung up, and Prateek was left with a queasy, ominous feeling in his stomach.

Any other boy's night would not have been acceptable to Megha, but that Saturday, Megha waved him away, the salad bowl in her lap, her eyes fixed on the television, *Grey's Anatomy* holding her attention.

Just as he was leaving, she said, 'I want to get pregnant after this summer.' Prateek paused, not turning. She stressed on the word, 'after'.

'Take me to a nice place. St Tropez or Miami.' She said it coyly, but it was a distinctly commanding tone.

He wondered if he could afford it. He would have to fly them business class at the very least, stay in rooms that would cost a thousand dollars, shopping that would be endless and expensive.

He smiled at her, 'Of course, Megs.'

'Have a boy's night now,' she said, her eyes returning to Patrick Dempsey.

At Gautam's house the party was taking shape. Balvinie, Laphroaig and a scattering of rare single malts stood indifferently on the marble bar counter. Between high fives and big-hearted hugs, in which he received many compliments about Gautam's new construction, he noticed two women, white, foreigners, clearly eastern European, exit the powder room. They were heavily made up, but dressed well in satin dresses, a touch revealing but not immodestly. Shit, he thought.

He had heard that Gautam sometimes indulged himself in Dubai or Hong Kong, with some of these guys, the richer ones, the ones who exported and travelled often, the ones who wouldn't agonize about a St Tropez holiday for their wives. But, he never confronted Gautam. There was scarcely a need to. It was Gautam's business and besides he would look like a prude.

The evening of cocaine and single malts sped on with two more women joining them, one who proclaimed herself as British Indian. She said she was a model, and talked in a posh accent about Delhi fashion week, her long legs crossed, her face upturned as she smoked a cigarette with Hollywood charm. Prateek couldn't take his eyes off her.

'Want her?' said Gautam whispering, but not really whispering, his voice audible enough, so that if she were listening she would have heard him. Prateek blushed and looked away.

'What? No,' Prateek said, pouring himself another drink, from a bottle he had never heard of, the ink signature of the malt maker spreading under his wet fingers. 'Sorry,' he said in the same sentence.

'Fuck that,' Gautam said pointing at the bottle, 'it's meant for drinking. But, fuck her.' He tilted his head towards the British Indian.

'No man,' Prateek said trying to keep his voice shy, sweet yet obedient.

'You got your period, Prats?' said another friend near the bar and Gautam roared with laughter.

Prateek took a deep breath, drank his glass empty and left.

For a week Prateek did not hear from Gautam. I shouldn't have left, he thought. That was childish. He speculated what to do and then dialled him.

'Hey,' said Prateek.

'Hey Prats,' said Gautam, 'in a meeting, I'll call you later?'

Of course he would be in a meeting, thought Prateek bitterly. Just because I didn't play to his tune. It's always Gautam's way or the fucking highway.

A few days later he hadn't heard from Gautam and heard he was travelling. New York, said Megha proudly, as she sat filing her nails in bed. He wondered if his wife would have such a crush on Gautam if she knew he was probably fucking some blonde whore in New York, sniffing cocaine from her tits.

Ten days went by. Other than the significant and desperate need to make up with his friend, this would not have mattered to Prateek. After all, it was only a matter of time before they met.

But by now he also needed his pending payments. Mr Chatterjee kept asking him for patience and time.

Mr Chatterjee was Gautam's accounts manager who handled payments. Prateek was glad to deal with Mr Chatterjee. It is embarrassing to talk money with a friend.

Prateek could afford the delay for the time being, but it enraged him that Gautam would hold his payment for not playing along that night. Just like him, he thought.

Let me ask Priya when Gautam is back, he thought. Dear Priya, he thought.

'He's back tomorrow, Prateek,' said Priya sweetly. When he hung up, he looked at his phone and thought, *Prateek … only Priya calls me that*. He repeated his name audibly, enjoying the sound of it.

Two days later, allowing for jet lag, he called up Gautam.

'Gautam, brother,' he said, his voice shaking.

'Yes bro,' Gautam answered, his voice evidently calm and businesslike. There was no acknowledgement that he had not returned Prateek's call. Of course he wouldn't, thought Prateek.

Prateek told him about the payments in sentences full of starts, stops, shifts and stammers.

'Bro, you've been dealing with Mr Chatterjee for six months now. Take it up with him. But, don't worry, I'll put in a word.'

Put in a word, Prateek couldn't believe it. The fucking bastard.

The next day, hoping to meet Mr Chatterjee on site, Prateek was pacing the driveway when Priya pulled up. She was driving herself.

'No driver today,' she said exiting the car. She was wearing dark blue jeans and a white shirt. White suits her, thought Prateek. She's beautiful. He dared his thoughts to go further.

They walked the site and she seemed more enthusiastic this time. He pointed at the few changes the architect had suggested, the new masonry, some added windows. His voice was melancholy, he couldn't bring himself to look at Priya.

'You've been just wonderful,' she said to Prateek. He looked at her gratefully. Before entering her car, she leaned up to him and kissed him softly on his cheek. Prateek swallowed as he watched the car drive away.

It was nearing July. Megha reminded him of their impending holiday plans.

Had he done their tickets? Had he booked the Byblos at St Tropez?

Yes, he answered to these questions.

Mr Chatterjee continued to ask for more time. Vexed and incensed, he decided to call a common friend to plead for a solution.

He had barely said hello when his friend excitedly told him that Priya was out of town once again and Gautam was having an impromptu boy's party that night.

'Really,' said Prateek and quickly hung up the phone after brief formalities.

He called Gautam. 'Hey man, can I come tonight? I heard from...'

'Of course Prats. I was just about to call you.'

Yeah right, thought Prateek. Fucking Liar. Tonight, I'll show him I'm just as much man as he is.

Readying for the evening, just as he had two months earlier, he was once again stopped by Megha at the door. The television was flickering; Patrick Dempsey was absorbed in surgery.

'Baby, we are leaving next weekend, right?'

'Yes, Megs,' he said sweetly, without turning.

At Gautam's house the scene seemed unchanged, as if this too had been paused, frozen in time, single malts, cocaine and women spilling from mouth, nose and lap.

Gautam gave him a big hug, apparently drunk. 'Man, I have been so fuckin' busy. It is so good to see you. Where have you been? Priya told me that you're at the site all the time. Don't sweat it so much man.'

It seemed like one long sentence. Yeah fucking right, Prateek thought. Don't sweat it so much!

Gautam continued, 'Brother, I am really sorry for your payment delay. I have no words. I was just too tight up this month man. I was too embarrassed to call. It will never happen again.'

Prateek glared at Gautam. He helped himself to the most expensive single malt, filling the glass to the rim.

'Slow down man!' shouted one.

'Check that out!' cheered another.

Prateek gulped it down to the sound of claps and hoots.

Glowering down Gautam Khurana, he took the British Indian's hand and kissed it theatrically. He started to dance with her, his hands on her waist, his hips pressed to her, his thoughts about Priya, her swaying white dress, the white shirt, the kiss she had given him. He touched his cheek at that spot and with that thought he took the model to an adjacent room.

Twenty minutes later he emerged, his shirt crushed, his hair unruly, and his breath steaming of whiskey. Hardly anyone noticed. They were intent on their own celebration, each singular in their purpose.

'Hey man, that was some show,' said Gautam, drunkenly but a hint of disappointment in his voice, disdain apparent in the way he held his shoulder.

Prateek looked at him warily. 'Well, I wanted to join the club.'

'You sure did man,' said Gautam. 'Never thought you'd be into this, Prats.' He tried to say his nickname lovingly but the dismay was barely masked.

'I never thought you were either, Gauti,' said Prateek his voice unsteady with whiskey and sex.

'Me?' said Gautam laughingly. 'Never brother. Just keeping up entertainment for these fools,' sweeping his arm at the depraved room. 'Priya's my Kohinoor, man. I couldn't ever do that.'

'And she loves you, Prats. She's just so angry at me for delaying your payment.'

Prateek was gulping down fistfuls of air, his eyes blinking hard and fast.

Gautam continued, 'I've told Chatterjee to clear your payment tomorrow. So fucking sorry.'

Thirty Seconds

The day before I turned thirty, I was sitting in my cubicle, tapping mindless emails. It was lunchtime and I was sitting with my colleague and somewhat friend, Mohit.

Mohit was talking about the party our friend Pia had organized for me that night. He was excited; there would be expensive champagne and perhaps quality cocaine. It was Saturday ... a perfect reason to get drunk. Saturday and my birthday.

I was distracted through the lunch. There was a fairy sitting on top of the credenza on the far end of the cafeteria talking quietly to herself. I had met her nineteen times before, but never outside my bedroom. I don't keep my windows open at night, so she didn't fly in. She just appeared. I never bothered to ask her how she did that. It never mattered to me as long as she kept coming back.

But on top of the cafeteria credenza she sat, looking a bit troubled, aware that I was looking at her, because she kept flashing coy glances as if she was quite unconcerned whereas her behaviour suggested otherwise. Mohit couldn't see her, so he kept talking to me about Pia, Pia's breasts, the party and cocaine. I only half listened.

When he got up to use the toilet, I walked over to the fairy quickly and said, 'Mika, what are you doing here?'

Mika wasn't her real name; in fact I didn't know what her name was. I only called her that because the first time she came to my room, I was listening to Mika on the radio, and when I asked her name, she shrugged and asked me to choose one. So Mika it was, and Mika seemed pretty and unisex and I think it suited her. Mika, my fairy, was tiny, just like what you see in the movies or read about in children's books.

She looked at me with large eyes, eyes in which – if you peered closely – you could see a swirl of brightly coloured specks moving around the pupil, not unlike the pictures one sees taken by the Hubble, pictures of faraway galaxies. She said in a voice that reminded me of unrequited dreams and secret desires, 'It's your birthday tomorrow Aditya, and I've come to grant you your wish.'

Your wish. Others must have wishes too, I thought.

This was the first I had heard of any wishes. To be sure, the first time she appeared I had immediately thought of wishes and lamps. For me, fairies and jinns are supposed to be about wishes, flying carpets, adventure and intrigue. A possible romance. Probably a rescue ... and a moral of the story. But she simply wanted to talk. That left me a bit distressed and disappointed. Having a fairy in my room was not enough. I am not easily satisfied.

But this does not happen to too many people. In fact I didn't know if it ever happened to anyone. I never told anyone about *my* fairy, and to be fair others never mentioned theirs to me – if they had a fairy that is.

I looked at her, equally puzzled excited and annoyed.

She mirrored my exact look, as she so often did, and said, 'You don't want it?'

'Sure, I do. Its three wishes usually, right? Is this some kind of a joke?'

'I'm a fairy, Aditya. Do I look like I need to joke with you?'

I didn't reply, but I did notice that she hadn't answered my first question.

The first time she came it had been for barely a minute. No sooner had I selected Mika as a name for her, she had vanished, leaving me wondering if I was hallucinating or perhaps she was a puppet or some kind of new-age Sony robot my friends were messing with.

When we met the second time it was obvious that she wasn't out of a Sony factory. She sat on my wrist, her legs crossed, her face cupped in her hands, her long eyelashes resting on her pink cheeks and as she listened to me, I realized that this was very real.

Every time she came she asked me to choose a subject, anything at all, and talk. At first I was more than intrigued by this instruction, but I obeyed. The rules were that I could talk as long as I wanted and on any subject, but I had to speak on that subject alone. This was not easy the first few times. She would shake her head as soon as I digressed.

But then I began to speak easily and I made no mistake, no digression. This way she taught me how to concentrate.

I wasn't sure how many of these sessions we were going to have, and I didn't want to know. I wanted the magic to continue.

It was astounding how soon I became dependent on her company, how impatient I was in the fifteen odd days between each meeting. It was mostly fifteen days, once it was even nineteen. Every time a fortnight passed, I couldn't sleep. I was always worried that she wouldn't come back, and I dared not ask her why she came only after fifteen days.

She had her rules for me, but apparently none for her.

Of course, I fell in love with Mika. Many a time I tried to dissuade myself, acknowledging that this was neither possible nor logical. I blamed my feelings on the recent break-up I had had with Diya, my girlfriend of nearly three years. Sometimes I would try to be aloof with Mika, but it was useless and pathetic.

I was sure she knew what I felt for her, as she sat on my wrist, leaning against my watch, her thick lustrous hair carelessly tickling my skin, her eyes looking so deeply at me, that she must know things about me that I did not.

Now, in the cafeteria, I simply did not know what to say.

'Well, do you think you need time to think?'

'Yes, maybe,' I said haltingly.

'I'll be back before your party. Think about it till then. Watch, your friend is back.'

And with that she vanished. I hadn't told her about the party.

I turned to walk back to Mohit, who remarked unkindly, 'Looks like you were talking to yourself Adi. Definitely turning thirty. Not easy, eh?'

I had wanted to tell someone about Mika for so long, that I nearly told him right then. I laughed and changed the subject.

I could not wait for the evening to come; I tapped a few more mindless emails, and floated about the accounts department even though I had no business there. Looking at the clock repeatedly, I ignored my work and left work by seven, two hours before my usual time.

Brushing past my mother who was busy baking a cake to take with me to the party, I ran up, taking three steps at a time, my mother hollering her disapproval, saying something about broken bones. I drowned her voice, closing the bedroom door with a back kick.

Mika was already there, sitting on my desk reading a book laid out in front of her. The page was turning magically. She looked up and said, 'Hello Aditya.' She never called me Adi, as all my friends and family did, and she used my name a lot in her sentences. I loved the way she said my name. It made an otherwise common name sound like it was the most special in the world.

'Beautiful book,' she said. She was reading my favourite author, Haruki Murakami.

'Mika, may I know your name please?'

'Is that your wish?' She smiled wryly.

'No.' Then pausing I said, 'Actually, why not?' .

She laughed, a laugh full of abandonment and freedom. It made her eyes twinkle, her cheeks full and her perfect mouth open, revealing bright white teeth.

'What's your wish?' She said sternly.

I looked at her and walked towards her, picking her up easily in the palm of my hand, and brought her close to my face. I took a deep breath.

I wanted to tell her how much I wanted her. How much in love with her I was. It didn't even matter if she wasn't a *person,* I was happy as long as she would be mine.

But I didn't.

It didn't matter. Of course she knew.

Instead I said, 'Let it be. It's great the way it is. I don't want a wish. I don't want anything. Keep coming like you do and that's good enough. That's my wish.'

She was silent for a few seconds. Her eyes never left mine. The galaxies were swirling gently. They looked blue.

'I can't do that. This is my last visit. I'm done with my work here Aditya. One wish, anything you want. Be careful, because it will come true. Tell me what it is and then let me go.'

Work.

I was some kind of assignment chosen by someone, something to have sessions with, the outcome of which I had no idea of. Was this a survey? Was I a statistic in a hypothesis?

I wanted to tell her that she could tick 'yes' in the part of the questionnaire which said, 'did participant fall in love with surveyor?'

But I didn't. I pursed my lips, letting them make a squeaking sound.

She suddenly disappeared. This happened sometimes without warning.

I got into the shower and turned the water to scalding hot. The bathroom was all fogged when I stepped out, my body red and burnt. In the steamed mirror, Mika was looking right back at me. She was on the other side. I was naked but I wasn't embarrassed. I was glad she saw me like that.

She was smiling. It was as if she was looking into a mirror herself.

I got ready, buttoning my shirt slowly, not once taking my eyes off Mika. Just as I could hear Mohit greeting my parents downstairs, Mika stepped out of the mirror.

'The wish, Aditya?'

I leaned over to her, my lips caressing her hair, taking in her beautiful smell that drove my senses mad, I found her tiny perfectly formed ear, and held her tiny perfectly formed hand as soft and small as a rose petal and pressed it against my chest and said, 'Make this go away.'

Almost immediately, as if she was ready with the answer, she said, 'I can.'

I looked at her quietly, my eyes stinging, a lump racing to my throat. I shook my head, and took her hand to my mouth and kissed it gently.

'Go Mika. Go.'

'Your wish, Aditya?'

'Does everyone fall in love with you Mika?' I said.

'Not like you did,' she said.

I looked in those unforgettable eyes for the last time before she vanished. Then my heart broke. The pieces fell against my ribs, stinging, hurting.

Mohit entered the room and yelled, 'Hey Adi. Getting late man. You look like hell. Told you turning thirty was not easy. Let's go.'